COLLECTIVE CHAOS

ELIZABETH SUGGS

JONATHAN REDDOCH

CONTENTS

MICHAELA RAE

THE AIR WAS thick and heavy with the scent of rain as Delilah dashed down the front steps of her dilapidated apartment building, its once-vibrant facade now faded and crumbling. Her brunette hair kept whipping into her face, but she quickly smoothed it out, her silver makeup glittering under the dim street light.

Sporting a silver mini dress, she accessorized with a headband adorned with two bright green pipe cleaners, each topped with a ping pong "eyeball" featuring a Sharpie-scribbled purple iris.

Her stomach jittered at the thought of her hunky farmer boyfriend as she got into her black Beetle. Things had been heating up between her and Sam for a while now. She couldn't wait to attend the costume party on his family's farm. Sam had been so sweet and attentive, making her feel like the luckiest girl in the world. Tonight, she secretly hoped, would be the night they took their relationship to the next level—one she'd remember forever.

As she sped down the road, she felt a mix of nervous energy and the warm buzz of the tequila shots she had hastily taken. Delilah didn't consider that the long and winding roads of her podunk town would look different during tonight's storm. She glanced down at her phone navigation, trying to steady her shaking hands on the wheel.

She glanced up, just as a little black cat dashed into the street. Jerking the wheel to avoid it, she slammed into a deep puddle, the tires hydroplaning across the slick asphalt. The vehicle lurched sideways with an unsettling screech, smashing into a nearby telephone pole. The pole wobbled, then fell forward, crumpling the trunk.

She looked out her cracked window at the night sky. The moonlight illuminated a rustic stable in the distance. A lamp flickered on.

Then, everything went dark.

———

Delilah woke to the sensation of warm liquid dripping onto her cheek. She reached up to wipe it away. Bright, sterile blue light flooded the room. She looked at her hand as thick blood slowly flowed down her fingers.

She realized then that she was lying naked on a sterile table.

Where am I?

Panic rose in her chest. Her heart pounded as she tried to make sense of the surreal scene.

Radio static sizzled and shrieked through a speaker system. It was a voice speaking a language unlike any she had heard.

Am I dreaming?

Out of the corner of her eye, she saw a translucent white tentacle slither into view, its glimmering under the harsh light. It wrapped around her forehead with a chilling, deliberate grip. She felt a burning sensation near her hairline, her bleeding wound sent jolts of electricity into her stomach as the horrifying realization washed over her that this was not a dream.

Waves of shock and terror overtook her as her body began to convulse. Before she could scream, a searing pain shot through her arm. Looking down, a thin needle-like protrusion piercing her skin. The alien technology worked quickly; paralysis took hold. Her heart raced as she fought to move, realizing only her eyes remained mobile. She peered down at her changed body. Her stomach was large and transparent, like the tentacle draped across her chest.

As her eyes adjusted, she noticed that there were thousands of steel tables around her, filled with clean, unconscious bodies of other naked, impregnated humans, varying in size and color.

The tentacle reared back and morphed into the form of Sam. Its screeching became Sam's sweet, familiar voice.

He whispered, his voice a sickeningly sweet echo of the man she thought she knew. "I am so glad you survived, Delilah. Now, our bodies can become one... welcome to the family farm."

SMART

JOSHUA G.J. INSOLE

MAYOR ROY BANKS towered over the podium, hands clutching the wood.

He beamed out at the enraptured crowd. Good people. *His* people. He had them right where he wanted them, in the palm of his hand. He stood before them as the ideal politician—perfect suit, great tie, coiffed hair. Re-election next year would be fine. Celeste Horton—with her ecofeminism rubbish—could eat it.

"… completely top of the line and ready to go! Whether it's our neighbors from the east or our neighbors from the west, when the crap hits the fan, we'll be safe."

The crowd cheered and hooted. The mayor basked in their praise. He held up his hands and mimed the words *thank you, thank you, thank you very much.*

Once enough time had passed, he cleared his throat and continued his speech. "It has all the mod cons. Everything we could ever need. Praying that nuclear war never happens, of course." A few mumbles of "of course" rippled through the crowd. "You'll never hear from your teenage son that he's bored while down in this bad boy." He slapped the metal wall next to the elevator doors. "Did someone say video games and

TV? When the time comes to re-emerge, your son won't *want* to leave!" That got a hearty chuckle from all the parents and sardonic eye rolls from the minors.

"We didn't spare a single expense!" An important fact to impart. When the question of where all the money went arose, Roy could point at this metal monstrosity and shrug. "I guess you could call it—" he did air quotes "—a 'smart' bunker." A few middle-aged men, obsessed with their toys and gadgets, raised their eyebrows. They pulled *well-I'll-be* expressions.

"And now..." The mayor took the oversized scissors from his assistant, Morton—a bald twenty-something. Morton smiled a rat-like grin at the audience. "I do declare that Gideon's Point fallout shelter is—" *snip* "—open!"

As luck would have it, the moment Roy cut through the ribbon, the town's air-raid siren sliced through the crowd. It rose—*wahhh*—and fell—*ohhh*—like the scream of a mechanical baby.

A few faces in the crowd frowned and glanced around. Some turned their gazes to the skies as if they could see the bombers flying overhead. But most continued to watch the mayor, convinced something special would soon occur.

Fate would prove them right.

He ran his hand through his hair and turned to his assistant. "Morton, is that a practice drill?"

Morton, sweat sparkling on his skull, tapped at the tablet he carried with him everywhere he went. Pages and images flashed as he *rat-tat-tatted* against the smudged and smeared glass. "Uh, n-no, sir, there's no practice run scheduled for to—"

Morton tapped the device again. He pulled a face and shook his head. "No. Nothing in honor of today's proceedings. Besides—" he flashed a smile that would curdle milk "—I would have known about it if it was. It appears that—"

The mayor ignored the rest of what Morton had to say. Instead, he turned back to the podium, where the audience—

his audience—remained frozen. They needed a leader, a shepherd. *Baa, baa, help us; we are but poor sheep.*

"All right, ladies and gentlemen." A snake whispered at the back of his mind: *Time to shine.* He loosened his tie. "Our opening of this shelter was most practical. According to my assistant, those sirens you hear are the real deal." With calming gestures, he soothed the panic, which bubbled up like boiling water from a pot. "Worry not." The mayor gave the town his winning grin, the one that he'd had plastered on every bus stop. "I'm here to guide you through it. Now, everyone, please follow me in an orderly fashion." He glanced at the officers at the edges of the mob, who nodded in affirmation. "We're going into the shelter."

The mayor turned and strode towards the shelter's elevator doors, the only way in or out of the bunker. Ultra-secure. Wide enough for two buses, side-by-side. Behind him, the sheriff and his boys corralled the crowd.

The sheriff said, "Yes, there's enough space for everybody down there. No, we won't run out of room. But, yes, everyone will get down there in time." And then the sheriff added something that made Roy take pause, "Look, there's the tech wiz assistant off to get things ready."

The tech wiz? Did he mean Morton? No, that couldn't be right. Roy should be the savior here, not his goddamn *assistant.* He barged Morton—who yipped like a Chihuahua—out of the way. "Let the *real* men handle this, Morton."

Before Morton could say or do anything, the mayor reached the elevator controls and blocked the view with his considerable bulk.

A small black control panel glinted in the sun, embedded into the wall next to the elevator doors. The blast doors remained closed and sealed—ready to withstand the might of whoever's army. The moment for him to remedy that had arrived. He pushed locks of his sweaty hair away from his face.

Roy raised a hand to the device, chubby fingers poised, and paused.

He frowned.

The control panel had no buttons—only a sleek onyx screen. It mirrored Roy's ruddy jowls inside its silver metal frame. "Wha—?" He peered from side to side. No buttons. None at all. None on the sides because the damn thing lay flush against the wall's surface.

Morton whisper-shouted at him, "It's touchscreen. You have to use your fingers."

"Why the hell would *this* need to be a touchscreen?"

"Sir, would you like me to—?"

"No, no! I've got this." And then, as if to himself: "I've got this." He swallowed hard, pulled his tie down even further, and undid his shirt's top button.

He reached out and prodded the screen. Nothing happened. The mayor poked it again and again, and still, nothing happened. He turned to Morton, eyes wide and white. "Why won't it—"

A happy jingle played through unseen speakers, and the panel screen flashed white. A heartbeat passed, and then words faded into view on the screen: *Welcome! Initializing first-time setup, please wait.*

Hot and wet sweat sprung out from every pore on his body. The mayor had to arm beads of moisture out of his eyes. He whimpered, "Awe, c'mon." For the first time in his mayorship, the public's gaze didn't fill him with a sense of well-being.

In the distance, someone yelled.

"What's taking so long?"

"We could get nuked any minute!"

Finally, the screen changed. *Welcome to your brand-new fallout shelter! Please complete the following steps to set up your account.* Below that, a button labeled *NEXT* lay in a blue bubble.

Roy tried the touchpad again and found that his sweat-wet fingers didn't even register on the device. "Aw, jeez." He rubbed his hands on the suit and wiped the sweat away. The mayor tried again. The blue button dipped inwards the way an actual one would. *Gee, how neat.*

But nothing happened.

A small circle appeared in the middle of the screen. It spun. Behind it, the same page remained, only grayed out.

Roy's frown deepened. "I-I don't—"

"Sir, are you sure you don't want *me* to handle this?" Morton's voice dripped with superiority. "After all—" he waggled his tablet at the mayor "—I am the expert in these things."

Sure, Roy *could* do that. But then, whose face would be on the cover of *Time*? His? Or—he shuddered—Morton's? If he lost control now, as the sirens wailed like a choir of banshees, he could kiss re-election goodbye. *A vote for Mayor Banks is a vote for incompetence!*

Another shout from the crowd: "If Horton was mayor, we'd already be inside!"

No! No!

Roy shook his head and snapped at his assistant. "I said I've got this!"

Morton raised his hands and his eyebrows, then took a step back. His head glistened like a polished bowling ball. His eyes glinted in their sockets.

Roy returned to the control panel. The page had—thank whichever god had decided to smite them with a nuclear attack—moved to the next. *Please select your internet connection.* Then, the words *WIFI* and *WIRED* shone in two blue bubbles beneath. The mayor hesitated, then chose *WIFI*. Everything ran on WiFi. Right?

The next page loaded much faster. The bunker had found a few in-range WiFi routers. But all of the connections—*It Burns When IP, Girls Gone Wireless, No More Mister WiFi*—had a padlock symbol. Roy closed his eyes and groaned. He turned to the crowd. Their eyes no longer showered him with adoration. Instead, their gazes ripped the flesh from his bones. He asked if anyone would let him share their internet.

"I'm not giving my WiFi password away."

"I ain't payin' for no freeloaders!"

"No way."

"I could get hacked!"

"People." The mayor gritted his teeth. The sirens continued to screech their sine-wave song. A migraine twinged behind his left eye. "If you could only understand that our lives depend on—"

An acne-faced teenager in a hoodie pushed his way to the front of the mob. He held his mobile phone aloft. "I can hotspot you, man."

A blonde woman with an *I-want-to-speak-to-the-manager* haircut elbowed her way to his side. "You will not, William. Your father and I pay a fortune for that blasted service! Do you know how much phone contracts cost? The fee for going over your data allowance will be astronomical!"

The teenager gave his mother an embarrassed look. "Mom! This is why I told you to get the unlimited plan!" And then, in a lower voice, "Quit embarrassing me." His eyes flicked from side-to-side.

The mayor stepped forward. "Ma'am? We'll reimburse you. But as for now—" he squinted at the heavens, still clear "—we have more pressing issues at hand." He ushered the boy toward him with a snap of his fingers. "Come here, son."

With a few rapid thumb taps that moved faster than Roy's eyes could comprehend, the boy nodded. "Yep, uh-huh. It's good to go."

"When should it—"

The page refreshed, and a new internet source joined the list. *Drop It Like Its Hotspot.* It, too, had a padlock next to it.

"Yeah, man, the passcode is *5318008*."

The mayor snorted. "I remember *that* one from my school days."

The teenager shrugged. "Whatever, gramps. Get us the hell outta here."

Roy wiped his fingers on his suit trousers and typed the code in. That blasted loading circle once more took center place. "Oh, for the love of—"

The jingle sounded again, and the page jumped to the next. Roy's eyes moved back and forth across the text, and his heart sank even lower. *Please create an account or sign in to continue.* Beneath: *CREATE A NEW ACCOUNT* and *SIGN INTO AN EXISTING ACCOUNT.* The mayor gritted his teeth and clenched his hands. His nails bit into his palms, hard enough to draw blood.

"What's the holdup?"

"Is he waiting 'til we hear the bomb whistling?"

"The man's falling apart."

Roy stabbed a finger at *CREATE A NEW ACCOUNT.* A form opened up. It asked for his name, age, gender, occupation, sexuality, and email address. "Morton." He spoke through clenched-together teeth. "What's my office email?"

"Oh." Morton smirked. "*Mayor Banks*—all one word. *At*—that's the little *a* with the circle around it. *Gideons Point*—without the apostrophe, also one word. *Dot*—that's a period. *Com*—that's Charlie Oscar Mike."

The migraine behind his eye throbbed. "Thank you, Morton." The fake smile on his face twisted his features like fire warps plastic. He jabbed his hand at the screen with reckless abandon. Any more shenanigans, and the blood vessels in his temples would pop. The mayor hit *SUBMIT.*

Please confirm your email address by following the link provided. Below that, a button that read *RESEND ACTIVATION LINK.*

Bile stung the back of Roy's throat. "Morton!" He clutched at the air in Morton's direction. "Check my damn email."

Morton nodded. His head sent reflections of light dancing. "Sir."

A heartbeat passed.

Two.

Three.

Four.

Roy's fingers hovered over the *RESEND ACTIVATION LINK* button. "Should I—?"

Morton shook his head. "No, give it a moment. Give it a moment."

The moment grew into an eternity.

"Morton? Morton!"

Morton's shoulders sagged. "Okay, you can—"

The mayor jabbed the button.

"No, wait, it's through!"

Roy blinked sweat out of his eyes. "But I pressed—" He gestured at the loathed screen.

Morton shook his head once more. "No, it's not working. Must have to wait for the new one to come in. *Ah*! There it is." He thumbed something on his tablet. "There. And if *I* know technology—and I do—then that should—"

The screen blinked into its next iteration. *Thank you! Please select your subscription type below.* STUDENT, PREMIUM, and *FREE TRIAL* sat in their respective blue bubbles.

The mayor slammed a fist against the shut elevator doors. His tie dangled from his neck like a half-tightened noose, and his damp hair lay in his eyes. "But I already paid for the damned thing! Why in the hell do I need a goddamn subscription! I—"

"Sir, sir!" Morton's eyes widened. He nodded his head in the direction of the crowd. Then, he spoke in hushed tones. "The public is watching."

Roy's stomach clenched, and he had to resist the temptation to void his bowels. Instead, he turned on his heel and faced the mob. They ate him alive with zombie gazes—they wanted to rip him apart. They jostled each other for places near the front of the crowd and lobbed questions and insults like grenades.

"Ah, a minor hiccup, ladies and gentlemen." The air-raid siren whined its doomsday call. "We'll—" He cleared his throat and reached to loosen his tie—but it already hung halfway down his chest. He undid a second button. "We'll be sitting in air-conditioned safety in no time." His voice cracked on the last syllable, but he didn't have the heart to repeat himself. The crowd continued to undulate, and the shouts persisted. Roy ignored them.

He faced the control panel once more and selected *FREE TRIAL*. A faltered heartbeat later, he yelled out, "Why do you need my credit card details for a free trial? This process is lunacy!" He kicked at the fallout shelter's sealed blast doors, yelped, and pulled out his wallet. Roy grumbled as he typed his details in, pausing now and then to dry his slaked hands on his besmirched suit. Finally, he hit the *NEXT* button.

Thank you!

The mayor smiled and sighed.

Rebooting.

His smile vanished. "What?"

The screen went black.

He slammed his fist again against the door. It made no sound.

"WHAT?!"

"Sir? I can take over. It's been a few minutes since the siren began, and we ought to start getting everybody down into the—"

"SHOVE THAT TABLET UP YOUR BACKSIDE, MORTON!" He thumbed his chest. "I'M THE ONE WHO'S IN CHARGE!"

Morton did a double take and flinched away from Roy. "I-I'm sorry, I—"

The mayor—hair a sweaty mess, tie clinging on for life,

shirt open to reveal a pasty chest— turned on the mob. Even the police, usually on his side, shuffled and stared at their standard-issue shoes.

"DOES ANYONE ELSE THINK THEY CAN HANDLE THIS BETTER THAN ME? HUH? DO YA?"

Crickets could have chirped in the ensuing silence.

"WHAT'S THAT? *NO?* WELL, THEN LET ME HANDLE IT!"

Roy swerved back to the control panel that would haunt his worst dreams—provided he lived long enough to dream again. The screen remained black, but white text flickered. *Installing updates 7 of 42 (16%), please wait.*

He screeched and pulled at the last few strands of his hair. "WHY DO YOU NEED TO INSTALL UPDATES? YOU ARE A DOOR AND AN ELEVATOR!" Roy punched at the wall, and something cracked. A flash of crimson sprayed the floor. He screamed and clutched at the bit from which bone protruded.

"Someone should take the lead, we're sitting ducks here!"

"Why don't the cops arrest him and put someone decent in charge?"

"Sir?" Morton hovered over his shoulder. "Do you need first aid? I happen to have taken a—"

Roy roared, "UP YOUR BACKSIDE, I SAID!"

Clutching his wounded paw, the mayor shuffled back to the panel. The digital deities saw fit to give him one goddamned break today. The rest of the updates flew by in seconds. When the screen pinged back on—with that jolly melody—Roy had to type in his password and username again. He winced and yelped each time he tapped the screen with his mangled hand.

And then—miracle of miracles—the doors shuddered open with a mechanical groan.

Roy scrambled inside as the mob behind him surged forward. He might survive until the elevator reached the bunker below. What happened down there would be anybody's guess.

They squeezed into the elevator, shoulder-to-shoulder. Not everyone could fit, but—hey—tough luck. If they had enough time, they'd send the elevator back up. Babies screamed. Women and children and men sobbed. The doors remained open.

The air-raid siren reached a fever pitch. It vibrated in every filling Roy had in his mouth.

Speaking of sending the elevator up and down, where were the buttons? The damn thing had no buttons on the *inside*, either. Roy raised his voice and shrieked over the din, "MORTON! MORTON, GODDAMN YOU! HOW DO I GET IT TO WORK?"

Morton, like a rat, crawled up through someone's legs and squeezed up against the mayor. He still clutched his digital tablet to his chest as though it could protect him from the blast. "Hi, sir! It's voice activated, you have to say *Hey, Ellie*—that must be short for elevator, right?—and then—"

Roy sucked in a deep breath, and then bellowed, "HEY, ELLIE! SEND US DOWN BEFORE WE ALL GET BLOWN TO SMITHEREENS!"

"I'm sorry, I don't know how to get to The Smithsonian. I am only capable of travelling between floors one, two, three, four—"

"HEY, ELLIE! SEND US DOWN TO THE BOTTOM FLOOR!"

"Would you like to go down to the bottom floor?"

Everybody in the elevator yelled as one, "YES!"

Everybody outside the elevator shrieked in terror, "NO!"

A momentary pause.

"I'm sorry, but it seems your weight capacity has exceeded one person. With our free trial, you are only permitted to test the functionalities of our services one at a time. To buy our

FRIENDS AND FAMILY package, please upgrade to our *PREMIUM* subscription. Upgrade now, and you can save—"

An explosion deafened them before they could hear the end of the elevator's sales pitch. The ground shuddered.

"Oh, sonofabit—"

The mayor's eyes melted into jelly, the skin blew away from his face, his skull fragmented, and his brains shot out like snot.

In other parts of the country, people descended into shelters the old-fashioned way, via the stairs.

And beneath the town of Gideon's Point, the new bunker survived the blasts without so much as a flicker of its lights.

BEYOND THE VINYL VEIL

ELIZABETH SUGGS

I CARVED a mark on my concrete bedroom wall. It was the seven hundred and twenty-eighth tally since the dirty air took over, killing almost everyone else. I had been one of the lucky ones who had heeded the modern prophet's warning. Jerome Phillips had warned of this impending doom, proclaiming salvation to those who bought his Wirly-Gig home Containment System.

My fiancée, Makayla, naive as she was, purchased the item off of a late-night infomercial. She bought one for her and one for me—the perfect isolation. I only wished we could have shared one, but being the traditional Episcopalian she was, she'd always believed living together came after marriage.

I used to stare outside at the red and brown haze, but eventually, my windows were so caked with grime that outside viewing became impossible.

I had been isolated for two years: no love, no outside, and no communication. Makayla had promised she would come, but that was before the lockdown started.

Every day I found mild comfort listening to the few remaining birds outside my window. Something desperately tapped against the vinyl outer covering until it broke the seal, releasing the pressure. A blackened bluebird scrambled in as the vinyl deflated, smacking into the clear glass pane. Peeping through the collapsing material, I expected a red and brown world, but instead, I saw a sprawling green oasis.

Perched right outside my window was a bluebird. It tweeted again as it tapped upon my glass until the window cracked and pieces of my protection fell away.

I leaped backward, bracing myself for the dirty air outside, only it wasn't dirty. The air didn't burn my throat or choke me like it was supposed to—like it did to everyone else.

Moving toward the window, the bird and I locked eyes. It chirped, its wings fluttering rapidly, then it flew away up into a deep blue sky.

I picked at a piece of the window, pulling out the shard as if it were a petal, and just like a flower, the shard seemed to carry the scent of lilacs, roses, and baby's breath. It was everything lovely about the world wrapped up in one small thing.

Outside, there were more flowers in dazzling, vibrant colors. I needed to see them, so I slipped through the window, spreading open the gap of my vinyl prison and dropping my feet onto soft green earth.

Above me, monkeys called and birds sang. Bees buzzed, and wind flowed like a gentle current around me. There were no yells or buses or harsh artificial green and red lights. This place was calm, welcoming. The light was soft and warm, the sun lightly dusting itself across my pale skin.

I walked through the forest, finding pleasure in the new sensations, the new sounds. I'm not sure how long I walked, but eventually, I came upon a cliff. It overlooked a valley of trees and greenery. There were no buildings, but there was one house: Makayla's.

"We will get married. We just need to wait this out," I remembered Makayla saying the day I locked my door. "I will visit you soon."

But soon never came. For once, I'd take matters into my own hands.

I climbed down the cliff with surprising ease and passed my neighbor Gloria. She sat on her porch, rocking in the noonday sun, smile plastered on her face. The world shifted slightly and became less green. For a brief, sickening moment, Gloria was a rotting corpse in the red haze of the world. But as soon as I turned away, the world became luscious and green just as before.

Makayla's house was a tranquil cottage in the midst of this green paradise. As I approached, a man in a white suit and head covering called after me. He looked like a beekeeper. He waved his arms up and down wildly. He was shouting, but I couldn't understand him. His words were muffled, like he was underwater.

Undeterred, I turned to Makayla's door. It was covered in the same vinyl shield as mine had been, but that was easily remedied—no need for that in this picturesque world.

"Makayla! I'm here. We can finally get married!" I called as the beekeeper sprinted toward me. I started to shout again, but the air turned sharp and metallic, cutting at my insides. I inhaled, then coughed. The world shifted again. That acrid air swirled around me and I saw my reflection in her window. My face was melting, but then I closed my eyes and drew in a heavier breath. When I looked out at the world again, it was bright and vivid with color. Makayla's face appeared in the window, horror-stricken.

"Don't worry, Makayla. I'm coming."

THE PRICE WE PAID

STETSON RAY

ONE AFTER ANOTHER, the cities of the world burned, and we did nothing. There was nothing we could do. Flee or burn along with them: those were our only choices. We barely made it out of Baltimore before the fires consumed the city.

My children are taking it pretty well, but my wife hasn't been herself since we left. Her face is pale, and her eyes are far away.

"Daddy, how long 'til we can go back home?" asks my youngest daughter, Hannah aged five.

"It could be a while, sweetie."

We drive on, the flames growing brighter behind us.

"If it rains and the fires go out, then can we go home?" asks my oldest daughter, Grace, aged seven.

"We'll see."

It could rain for a thousand years and the fires wouldn't be extinguished, but they're too young to understand that. They have no idea how bad it really is.

"Does that mean 'yes,' Daddy?" Hannah asks. "If it rains, can—"

"No more questions," my wife, Ellen, interrupts.

We ride in silence for a long time. The radio isn't worth

listening to; newscasters telling us how we're going to die? No thanks.

Some people think the government will put out the fires and save us, but that can't be true. It's too late. The leaders of the world are all tucked safely underground, waiting for the flames to extinguish themselves while we suffer. Will there be anything left when they finally emerge from their bunkers?

Probably not.

Do they care?

Probably not.

We pass a group of men walking beside the highway. They shuffle along like zombies, heads bowed. When they see us, they come to life. They try to flag us down. One waves his arms over his head and stumbles into our lane. My foot never leaves the gas pedal. The man moves out of the way, then throws something at us as we speed past him. It thumps against the side of the minivan. We keep going.

"Who was that?" Hannah asks.

"Nobody."

"Why was he in the road?" Grace asks.

"He just was."

Vehicles fly past us, some going well over a hundred miles an hour. People are fleeing the city. Nobody wants to stay and burn. The ship is sinking, and everybody is trying to stay out of the water for as long as they can. We're all looking for somewhere safe to go. Will we find refuge? It doesn't seem likely.

We're made for traveling, humans. We're always searching for some place new, never content with where we are. We spent thousands of years sailing the seas and walking the Earth, and once our home planet was conquered, we became restless. We looked to the heavens. First the moon, then nearly seventy years later, Mars.

But exploring the cosmos using rocket ships wasn't feasible —it was too expensive, and took too long to get anywhere—so a few years after we landed on the red planet, we gave up on traditional space travel. The world governments defunded their space programs and put their money toward other technology. We began looking at things in a different way.

It wasn't long before a team of scientists working for a tech company in California made a breakthrough. Suddenly far away worlds were within our grasp. Humanity reached out and touched the stars—but it cost us.

It probably cost us everything.

Sitting in the backseat, my girls are starting to look scared. They need something to keep them occupied. An idea pops into my mind.

"Does anyone want to play a game of I spy?"

My girls squeal in agreement.

"I'll go first. I spy with my little eye, something green."

"A tree!"

"Nope."

"Grass!"

"Try again."

"A sign!" Grace cries, pointing at a road sign for Richmond.

"That's right, now it's your turn."

Grace says, "I spy with my little eye, something—"

"How about I take a turn," Ellen says, cutting our daughter off. "I spy with my little eye, something red. Something growing. Something destroying everything we ever—"

"That's enough."

The van is quiet.

The game is over.

We continue down the road.

We're fortunate to still have a vehicle; some people got rid of theirs when the Travel Stations first opened. The government built them in every major city, airports of the twenty-first century. They became commonplace overnight, and for good reason: you go to a Travel Station, they stick you in a tube, and in a flash, you're transported anywhere in the world instantaneously, safe and sound, no side effects.

Or that's what they told us.

We sent explorers to every moon and planet in our solar system, then we set our sights on the rest of the galaxy. We shot people throughout the universe, along with everything they would need to start new colonies.

We found worlds similar to earth. We found worlds that shared nothing in common with our planet other than the basic shape. Glass planets. Lava worlds. Moons made of silver and gold and every other precious mineral you can think of.

The cost of traveling plummeted. We took a vacation to Italy. Then later the same year, we went back, just because we could. Traveling became cheap and easy. Shipping costs went down. The need for trucks and trains to transport goods disappeared. The real-estate market crashed and had to be rebuilt from the ground up. There was more to go around than there ever had been. The future seemed bright.

Then the fires started.

They were small at first, as small as atoms, but they quickly grew larger. Each time we sent someone or something across space, a hole opened—it just took us a while to realize it. The fires consumed everything, any type of matter, any type of space. They grew bigger and hotter until everything around them caught flame.

It happened very quickly.

Now the whole world is burning.

"Where are we going, Daddy?" Grace asks.

The question lingers in the air, a troubling pest. There is no answer. There is no plan. Get away from the fires: that's our only goal. After that... there's no use in worrying about it. We've got a full tank of gas and enough food to last us a week. We have time. It's not over yet.

Ellen is getting worse; she seems to be drifting away, separating from the world around her. Her fingers are cold. My lips touch the back of her hand, but she doesn't seem to notice. Hannah begins to cry and Grace joins her. Not long after, tears are rolling down my face. We cry until we're done. There's nothing left to do but drive.

We pass a sign that reads, "Harter Lake State Park."

"You guys wanna check out that park?"

My girls love the idea.

"Don't you think we should keep going?" Ellen asks, her voice practically a whisper.

"We should be safe. We're at least a hundred miles from the city."

The orange light is still glowing in the rearview mirror, but it's faint and far away. It's easy to pretend it will never reach us, at least for now.

We take rural roads as they are less crowded than the Interstate. No one else is around, no one mowing their yards or tending their gardens. The world seems dead. It doesn't take us long to reach the park. It's odd to see such a picturesque place devoid of people. There are no fishermen standing near the edge of the emerald green water, no children at the playground, no senior citizens speed-walking down paved paths that weave between a swath of ancient oak trees.

We pile out of the van and head toward a picnic table near the edge of the lake. We move deliberately, a procession of mourners.

It's so quiet it makes my head hurt.

The wind blows, and with it, comes a faint smell of burnt ozone, overheated electric matter. We eat in silence—ham sandwiches and potato chips. There's nothing to say. My girls still don't understand. They think we're moving. How are you supposed to tell your kids it's all over and there's nothing left to do except die?

How many more lakeside picnics will we have together? There's no way to know. This is probably the last one, but it's impossible to enjoy.

Ellen isn't eating. She's staring across the lake, a grave expression on her face.

The wind blows.
The burnt smell is stronger.
The sky to the east is orange, the clouds black.
We don't have long, but that doesn't matter.
Either the fires will burn themselves out, or they won't.
There's nothing we can do about it.
I just wish we had a little more time together.

MONARCH

JENNIFER LEO

"GRANDMA!" Harley screamed, "what's wrong?"

She looked at him with tear-filled eyes and whispered, "Monarch."

"How could this happen? We live in the city. Concrete surrounds us for miles."

"I went out to the green zone. I had to do a ceremony for your mother. I'm getting too weak now, Junie. I'm losing too much blood. If I go to the clinic, or someone sees me, they'll come for me."

"I won't let that happen!"

"I tried to do a healing ceremony, but I can't sing anymore." She held up her blood-spotted hands.

"What can I do, grandma?" he sobbed.

"I need a healing song: 'Place of Hidden Water.'"

"I don't remember that one."

"In that case, I need you to hike up to the mountain and look for the white flowers with yellow and pink centers."

"The flowers can help you?"

"If you go now."

He ran to his room and immediately stuffed a glass bracelet

into his backpack. He ran back to her room and tried to hug her, but she put her hands up.

"I'll be back in a day."

He didn't want her to see him bawling the way he did when he was her little Junebug. He would come to her with his face swollen and salty, and she would take him up in her arms and say, "What is it, my Junie; what has turned the sky for you?"

No matter what the trouble was, a skinned knee, a lost pet, a broken toy, she would have him laughing and smiling in minutes, and he would be ready to face the world again.

When he reached the old interstate entrance, he saw an electric scooter propped near a camp of nonconformers. These people moved in and out of the green zone, an uncontrolled area where Monarch was still rampant.

Capable of surviving for months in soil or leaves, *Ophryocystis elektroscirrha*, was actually a parasite, known to be deadly to Monarch butterflies for decades before the first human infection was discovered. It hit the suburbs of North America first. All those pristine rose gardens and flower beds became havens for the parasite. It started as a simple runny nose, followed by diarrhea. But eventually, every orifice would be hemorrhaging blood. It was a terrible way to die.

He stole the scooter and took off before anyone could protest. He told himself he was just borrowing it.

As he headed west, the sun setting in front of him. He chased the light.

He arrived an hour before sunrise. He overlooked their ancestral valley called Hidden Water. The painted desert layers told stories of eons in the making. The vibrant orange spots reminded him of the Monarch butterfly's wings.

As he watched the rocks, the sage, the brown earth and the sky around him, he noticed something small, glinting in the air. It moved towards him as though it was hopping on puffs of wind until it was finally close enough for him to see the brilliant orange and black wings of a monarch, a rarity as people have been destroying them for thirty years. It fluttered around a cluster of rocks, to a patch of desert grass, laden with delicate white flowers.

As he watched the butterfly extract nectar from the pink and yellow centers, memories flooded his mind. He could hear his grandmother singing a song that he thought was a dream. She was sitting by his bed, putting a cool cloth on his head and telling his body how to get well. That was why she had sent him there, not for the flowers, for the song. He knew the healing song! He just had to remember how to find it.

He sang the song through a few times.

Here we are
　Here to sing to you
　We know you have a struggle
　But remember that you were well
　Remember that you know how to be well.

It was an elegant combination of a melody and a prayer, full of life and hope.

It was morning when he reached the city. The sun had already climbed out from behind the cliffs to the east, and the concrete forest was alive with daily activity. He dropped the scooter at the base of the steps to autocharge and hurried inside.

Her door was open, and she lay still on her bed with her eyes closed, body stiff, and vibrant red trails of blood trickling down her face. Something about it was beautiful, almost like she was wearing sacred paint for a death ceremony.

He bowed his head and sang the song for her, to let her spirit know that he understood. That he had learned how to keep this part of her and their traditions alive.

. . .

We will stay with you
Our love will spread
With love you feel the healing
And then you will be strong again
And we will be with you.

He carefully wrapped her body in a thick wool blanket and with the scooter, headed out to the green zone. He placed her on a pyre and gave her a ceremony that lasted through the day. He sang all the songs he had rediscovered on his journey. He recounted stories she had told him and told her stories of his own life that he never had a chance to share. Finally, he gathered up her ashes and placed them in a canvas flour sack.

———

He let her ashes fly free with the wind in Hidden Water.

As he stood there, milling over lifetimes of memories, a butterfly flitted past his face. Then a new song came into his mind. It was not one that he could remember from before, but he felt like he knew it. He sang it out and the butterfly rose up and seemed to dance on the autumn breeze, before it flitted away.

He looked once more toward his family home, then turned to the east. She was home now, and it was a long way back to the city. He began the descent into the next valley, and as he walked, he sang his new song.

LUMINOSITY

MORGANA PRICE

DR. DAWN ZILLA was usually one of the first to arrive at the office. Her job, specifically, was to monitor the sun's luminosity and run simulations for any minute change that could occur in order to warn her higher-ups who worked with the government and such to make preparations for anything catastrophic. Others near her watched the growth of the sun's envelope, the internal temperature, predictions of flares, and so on.

Dawn took a sip of coffee as her computer booted up. She gasped as the too-hot liquid dribbled out of her mouth and off her chin. She inhaled sharply through clenched teeth.

"Really?" she grumbled as she wiped her chin with the back of her head. "You'd think this would've cooled a bit during the drive here."

Annoyed, she set the coffee cup aside and glared at it momentarily before returning her attention to her monitor.

Her cardigan clung lightly to her back and shoulders. She shrugged and tugged at it almost without thinking.

Sweat trickled down her back as she fanned her face briefly with her hand. More sweat dripped down her back. Her gaze drifted to the widget displaying the current temperature: *113°*

F. That hot this early? It wasn't even 7 a.m. She plucked at the collar of her cardigan a few times to circulate the air better.

A beeping alarm on her monitor grabbed her attention. The percentage of the sun's luminosity increased at an unprecedented rate. This shouldn't be happening for another billion years.

A bright flash erupted across the sky. She spun her chair away from the window, clamping her eyelids shut at just the right time. The building swayed as if the Earth shuddered.

Screams of panic filled the observatory.

"My eyes!" a coworker shrieked from somewhere in front of her. "I can't see!"

Dawn tumbled out of her chair and onto the floor. What she'd always known as a rather cold imitation-marble floor scalded the palms of her hands as she crawled toward the closest teleporter.

Cries continued to ring out in the most haunting of screeches.

Dawn squinted, barely opening her eyes even a sliver to see where she was going. She caught a glimpse of another coworker writhing on the floor in front of her. His eyes were completely gone, only smoking eye sockets remained as his skin and face bubbled and boiled.

She held in a gasp as she fumbled to her feet. The teleporter wasn't too far. If she wanted to survive, she'd have to sprint through the maze of melting people and equipment. Her shoes stuck to the ground. Her skin felt like she was on fire. The smell of burning meat, melting plastic, and singed hair made her gag almost uncontrollably. Peering through her eyelids, she noted that she was only a few quick strides from the teleporter's doors.

She flung herself after the rubber soles of her shoes had melded themselves to the floor.

She didn't budge.

Yanking each foot from her shoes, she screamed as her skin

seared to the floor. She used her momentum to propel herself, leaving a thin layer of cooked, dead skin with each step.

Crashing into the teleporter, she grabbed the hem of her shirt to hold the handle and yank the door open. She slammed the door closed and frantically poked the button on the teleporter's destination request panel.

Due to the tinted door, she was able to barely make out the inferno around her, yet she still saw blurred and wavy images of flames, wobbling blobs of flesh, and everything melting.

At this rate, Mars would surely be too close to the sun's envelope to be habitable.

A coworker's cooked body collapsed against the teleporter's door.

Dawn screamed as their face melted off their skull as they slowly slunk to the floor. She pounded the request panel.

"E-e-e-en-en-en-ter or ssss'-st-state the d-destination-ation," the teleporter's computer requested in a broken and staticky voice.

"EUROPA!" Dawn hollered, praying that the teleporter still functioned properly enough to send her there in the intense heat. Her charred skin crackled as she spoke and waited. Inside the teleporter, it felt like an oven.

Another flash of light forced her eyes closed. The industrial-strength tinting of the teleporter's door was the only thing keeping her eyes from burning out of her skull. A moment of gratitude flooded her chest only to be replaced by the heavy weight of dread as her eyes darkened, and her skin went numb.

A brief moment of nothingness brought tranquility to Dawn's particles as they sprinted through cold space, away from the sun's expansion.

A small beep barely registered in her ears as she tumbled into the teleporter's door on the other side. The door opened automatically, concluding the teleportation process. Her transport to Europa's science base was a success.

A cacophony of voices pierced through her damaged eardrums. The teleporter on Earth may have shielded her briefly from the sun's wrath, yet it still cooked her medium rare, leaving her steaming body with charred, hairless skin. Stick a fork in her; she was done.

"Oh, my God!" someone said.

Dawn was sure that individual called out to others, but everything was muffled around her.

"She's the only one that came through. The teleporter's malfunctioning."

"Does it have to do with the sudden expansion?"

"Of course, it does! Can you *not* see how big the sun is from here? If the sun hasn't already engulfed the earth by now, surely everything on the planet's surface is vaporized."

Dawn didn't recognize the voices of those who spoke around her. She had only been to the Europa station once before. It was unbearably cold that time, even under layers upon layers of protective clothing and anti-radiation shields around the facility to protect it from Jupiter, the sun, and any other rogue radiation.

She couldn't open her eyelids. She felt hands lifting and helping her

"Who are you?" someone asked to her right.

Beeping sounded to her left. "I can't scan the chip in her watch… it's too damaged," someone else answered.

"Mmm?" was all she could force out of her lungs and throat. "Doctor," she wheezed. Her lungs crackled with each shallow breath. "Dawn." How was she still alive? "Zilla."

"Can someone help me carry Dr. Zilla to the infirmary?"

Dawn used every ounce of her strength to speak. "Sun."

"What?" the person lifting her asked.

"Lum…" Her throat garbled. "… minosity." Coughing, her lungs erupted in searing pain. "Increasing!" She nearly fainted in agony. The skin on her face cracked and flaked off as her facial muscles stretched from talking and screaming.

"We know; it still is."

The sun's end-of-life cycle was ahead of schedule by nearly ten billion years. If it continued at this rate, it'd become a Red Giant Star in no time, melting the ice of Europa, creating a water world. In the station's current state, no one would survive the plunge.

A giant cracking sound erupted through the station followed by a massive moonquake, causing her to be dropped. It was already happening.

Her mind blanked. The gravity of Europa, Jupiter, and the other celestial bodies seemed to pull at her chest.

She imagined the cooling sensation of the thawing Europa water on her cooked form. Perhaps, she should've just stayed in bed this morning, where the air conditioning in her tiny living quarters was broken, but roughly at the perfect temperature.

THE WORLD AFTER TOMORROW

JONATHAN REDDOCH

THE INTERNATIONAL TERA PLANE ASSOCIATION'S remaining crew gathered around yet another body collapsed in the barren Antarctic tundra.

Greeedo112 was another victim of the most hostile climate on the planet. Endless plains of the merciless frigid dominion!

"Sh-should we bury him?" asked Ralph. The retired welder was hardy but not accustomed to traversing the polar environment. He knew little of the survival tactics needed to venture into the heart of the icy giant and pass beyond the great encircling wall. He did, however, earn his position on the team by partially funding the research operation with money raised through a reverse mortgage.

"No..." said Rickles, the amateur physicist and replacement field leader, "from here until the edge, we leave all dead weight behind." He was originally the third in the chain of command, and it was his advanced solar and lunar calculations that served as the impetus for the expedition to reach the ice wall.

The others bowed their heads solemnly, and each kicked a symbolic bit of frozen dirt over their fallen comrade. Rickles reached into Greeedo112's bulky coat and claimed his rations and knife. A mobile device slipped out and cracked on the icy surface.

"Does anyone know his real name?" asked Brett, the outsider, the "fake news" journalist.

The three other survivors shook their heads. The team only knew him from the flat-earther chat room. Greeedo112 was an especially paranoid conspiracy theorist. He feared CIA moles would go to any length to sabotage the expedition, maybe even going after their families.

Brett picked up Greeedo112's device and quietly tucked it away in one of his many deep pockets. Taking one last look at the blue corpse, he felt like he was looking into his future.

Brett had been embedded with militant rebels in the mountains on a hit-and-run campaign, accompanying drug cartels in their sales operations. He even went undercover in a human trafficking scheme, but he never felt this certain of death.

He fully accepted the high probability of dying on this ill-conceived, poorly planned, terribly executed expedition to the South Pole, but the fear of his story being lost in this frozen wasteland was still his greatest concern.

He gently tapped his pocket to make sure his field notes were secure. Part of that groundbreaking story would include the daily log kept by Greeedo112 and his predecessor Winston "Dark" Cavalier. Brett needed to make sure he was able to write his article and make sure it was recovered postmortem: he didn't want his chance at winning the Pulitzer lost in transmission.

The team shuffled off. Not before Greeedo112 suddenly stirred. Rising halfway, he pointed at Saria, the only real scientist in the group. "Some truths are not worth the peril! Turn back now; you can't unsee what the lens has deemed unknowable."

He then fell back lifeless, and his head shattered on a rock.

"Wh-what sh-should we do now?" asked Ralph to their leader.

Saria knelt and examined their twice-dead comrade. "I think perhaps his brain was suffering from the immense cold. It's likely the same will occur to us if we don't turn back."

Saria was a laboratory researcher during the day. But she also dabbled in cosmology and astrology on the weekend. She considered herself open-minded and god-fearing. Something big was out there; she was certain of that fact.

Rickles urged the intrepid explorers to keep moving. "We brave few, we will be heroes among mankind."

———

In the relative comfort of his tent, Brett ruminated on the psychology of conspiracy theorists that he researched in preparation for the expedition: they frequently suffered from delusions of grandeur, held an over-valued sense of self and of their place in the world, and clinged to an oversimplified world view.

Saria unzipped Brett's tent and entered unannounced. Her presence had invited a stiff chill that hit him to the core.

"I'm interrupting," she said, noticing his notes laid out carefully, which flapped with the wind.

As the group's resident pariah, Brett had never received visitors in his tent. Greeedo112 had publicly accused Brett of being an obvious plant from the "High Cabal." The team's original leader had allowed Brett to join their expedition but made it clear he was never to be trusted.

"It's fine," he said, quickly packing up his papers.

"May I?" she asked, pointing to a series of handwritten pages of calculations.

"Certainly," he said, handing his treasures to her. "I can't make heads or tails of that incoherent... gobbledy—" he said, realizing his audience was sympathetic to gobbledygook.

"No, this isn't gobbledygook," she said with a smile, "it's gibberish!"

She handed it back to him and thanked him for sharing. "What happened today... was—"

"Otherworldly?"

"I was going to say disheartening."

"Yes, yes. That too. Sometimes it's easy to lose the human element to the story."

She examined the unruly mass of papers until she found a star chart that had been Dark Cavalier's. She compared it to a chart she pulled from her stash of folded documents.

"According to my calculations, we are actually much closer to the Glacier Barrier than was originally predicted."

"We are?" Brett chuckled, "Well, finally some good omens."

She smirked. "Ralph's making supper if you want to join us."

"In a minute. I have some research I want to finish." He looked at the secured mobile device.

She nodded, "Make sure you eat to keep up your strength." She smiled. "And I saved this from Ralph's stew." She handed him a baggie containing Greeedo112's crystalized eyeball. He thanked her profusely for her generosity.

Smiling wide, Brett aimed Greeedo112's eyeball to unlock the chunky mobile device. He transferred over the daily log before the battery could die. Some excerpts below from Greeedo112's online Open-Mind Journal.

Brett read the daily log of Greeedo112's last day:

I know what the papers will say, what that reporter will say:

"Died of exposure."

But my friends, my true friends, will know the truth. No one from Minnesota dies of "exposure." Still another few miles left to the "scientific" research center, and my body is about to give way. But my resolve couldn't be stronger.

There is a traitor in our midsts. I am sure of it. Nothing else could explain our frequent mishaps, getting off course, and this sinister spirit of dire warning urging us to abandon our cause. From the CIA or the FBI, perhaps. I asked Rickles to investigate. I think tomorrow I die. He suspects the reporter. But I think it's the "scientist" Saria.

———

"Is that an iceberg?" asked Ralph, shivering.

"In the middle of the snowbank? No, it looks like a relay station," said Rickles calmly.

"Another, or the same one we passed days ago?"

"Maybe. Let's investigate," suggested Saria, always eager to explore.

Brett spoke up, "Well, according to this map—" but Rickles tore the map from his grasp.

"I trust that map as far as I trust the 'news' media," he said.

Brett stood his ground as Rickles blocked his path. The others stopped. None had the energy to intervene.

Brett reached for his map. Rickles held it out of reach. Saria admonished the standoff with an intense stare.

Finally, an exhausted Ralph said, "Hey, we don't have time; let's check out the station, and then make a plan."

The group pressed stiffly on. All enthusiasm was flushed from their frozen lips. Single file, they shuffled on into the blinding light of morning until they met the small white building.

As they approached the building, they encountered two massive signs written in a dozen languages: *Chemical Research Zone. Access Prohibited. Do Not Pass This Point.*

"Shouldn't we just go around? I don't want to get cancer," Brett said.

"Cancer is a hoax," Saria said.

Ralph raised a pickax, Saria raised her pistol, and Rickles raised a small useless pocketknife.

"Should we knock?" asked Ralph sheepishly.

"Oh, for heaven's sake!" Saria stepped up to knock before the shed's only door burst open. A man in a gray jumpsuit fired a machine gun at the interlopers, striking Rickles in the chest.

Saria shot the man in the gray jumpsuit, then Ralph stabbed her in the shoulder.

"Traitor!" Rickles lunged at Ralph, both landing in the snow.

Brett went for the dropped machine gun.

Ralph sprang on top of Rickles, beating him senseless. Ralph said, "You're all under arrest!"

"Freeze!" shouted Brett. Ralph stood up, raising his arms.

It was only then, in the stillness of the moment, that they became aware of the woman in a gray jumpsuit inside the tiny building: "Repeat, we have skeletons loose in the white quarter. We have skeletons—"

Brett aimed the gun at the transmission equipment as Saria cried, "Wait, Brett! What if we need to call for..."

It was too late. Brett destroyed the transmission equipment, sending the guard flying backward. They tied up Ralph and the female guard.

"What are you hiding?" demanded Brett.

Ralph laughed, "We don't know. But no one is allowed to see what lurks on the other side. If the truth got out about the nature of the world, it would be catastrophic for mankind."

Brett shook his head vigorously, "The truth is all that matters to mankind."

"I was wrong about you," said Rickles before succumbing to his wounds and passing out.

"I was wrong about me, too."

Brett tied up Ralph beside the shed to freeze, while Saria tended her shoulder wound. They dragged the guard into the shed, allowing him to die inside with Rickles, who was set up in a bed with drugs and food to keep him sustained for a while.

Behind the shed was a snowmobile, but they could not get

it to start without the keys. Brett and Saria left on foot for the final leg of their weeks-long journey.

———

As they rested, Brett perused some of his old research documents. How had he gotten into this mess? He returned to the beginning: the message boards.

Greeedo112: *How to prove them wrong. How to educate with evidence? When they don't listen to reason and instead follow false prophets, deceivers?*

Dark_Cavalier34: *only a fool thinks the world is round*

MarselMarsel69: *Yeah, fly to the moon yourself, stable genius.*

Live_&_learn:): *Kill yourself. Then fly around as an angel and report back as a ghost!*

MarselMarsel69: *Or just KILL yourself...*

Gutpunch666: *To the moon, alice!*

OnetimeChad: *Bro, I think you ned go on a trip around the world.*

Gutpunch666: *aROUND the world!*

Donothan_Rickles: *You need HARD evidence, if they not follow logic. I will journey to the outter wall. I will prove them all wrong. To mount the expeidition of a lifetime and to be heralded as THE saviour of all humankind. I will show them all.*

Gutpunch666: *Go to the south pole and prove em all wrong.*

Greeeeedo112: *Haters. All of them. They knew not the challenge they brought forth. The stabilized geniuses of the world can't let the hater loosers get them down. We owe it to society to use our minds for the greatest good: knowledge.*

Donothan_Rickles: *Not all of us. I have been doing some research and your theory is correct. I have drawn a map that leads to the edge of the world and the great wall and the drop off. They must not want us to know about it. I will help you plan this trip!*

Greeeeedo112:*Thank you! We will do this and prove them all wrong.*

Simple-Saria: *I think you are 10000% right! I will join your epexdeition to.*

Brett_the_jet: *I am a reporter for the Daily Investigator. I would like to tag along on your trip. If you are correct, this is a discovery worth documenting.*

———

They stumbled forward through the white mist until they nearly struck it: the mammoth structure. The only wonder of the world left undiscovered.

The wall of porcelain was smooth and unclimbable. How could they possibly breach such a surface?

Saria was overcome with emotional exhaustion. She fell to her knees. "After all this."

Distraught, the two leaned on each other. One, a believer, the other, a skeptic: both without evidence.

Their pity party was eventually interrupted by a low hum of a snowmobile.

"The guards! They found us," Saria said, raising her weapon.

"What's the use now? There's nowhere to run."

"But the world needs to know the truth," Saria said.

"What truth? We don't even know the truth!"

As they argued fruitlessly, the snowmobile approached.

To their surprise, Rickles dismounted the vehicle and buckled in the snow. The pair ran to help him up.

"I found a weather balloon in the monitoring station," Rickles said.

Brett and Saria managed to get the balloon airborne.

Up, up they flew until they hovered over the peak of the barrier and secured the line. They disembarked the balloon.

First, Saria approached the edge.

She leapt for joy and screamed. "Hurry, guys. You won't believe it. I can't even describe it."

Brett reached Saria.

Saria clapped in giddy euphoria, teetering precariously close to the precipice.

"The truth, Brett. All I've ever wanted is the truth, wherever it may lead."

"That's great, but you're standing too close to the edge. Step back." He held out his hand.

"Science, religion, philosophy, alternative facts," she continued, "none of it ever panned out. It was all wrong."

She leapt over the edge with a glorious smile on her face.

"Saria!" he screamed. In shock, Brett reached for the falling body.

After a minute of weeping into his hands, he turned to Rickles. "My god, Rickles, your eyes! What the hell did you do to yourself?"

Rickles face was drenched in blood, oozing out of his empty sockets. In one hand, he held his multi-tool and the other his eyes.

Rickles replied in a voice not his own, "I won't be needing these to see any longer, or this—" He laughed and cut out his tongue. His mortal frame collapsed and fell backward over the inner edge of the wall.

What madness could lead to such an end?

Brett's extreme curiosity overcame his horror. He slowly edged himself to peer over. He braced himself and then shuddered. For the first time in his short pointless life, he saw.

What did he see?

He saw us. *The* us.

He saw himself. He was reflected in the lens of the boundless eye.

He saw the link among all humanity, minuscule specks riding the incomprehensible colossus that expands the unknowable universe.

He saw the past, present, and the future: the history of our world written in the blink of the twilight eye.

He saw the divine devourer. The great and spacious maw. The undulating tentacles of ubiquitous displeasure.

For the spiraling disc we call earth is only but one member in the great whole that comprises all things both living and dead.

The circular structure that blocked our view of reality protected our fragile microscopic sanity; he saw that now. The earth was a mere cellular unit, one of billions, whose purpose was microcosmic and lifespan indeterminate. Just a mere skin flake on the surface of the universal beast.

He had stared at the void, and the void noticed him not.

What would Brett do? What could he do? What does the mite upon the burro's back do when confronted with its own mortality?

Would he succumb to existential nihilism as Rickles? Or the deranged insanity of Saria, now a victim of her own obsession.

What would the mite do?

It matters not as humanity lay at the cusp of annihilation.

DIVIDE AND CONQUER

ROBIN KNABEL

GAME MASTER HOYT stands just out of reach of our enclosure. Spitting at us through the iron bars, he laughs as we dodge his phlegm. His ratty old prison guard uniform is baggy, and the pistol in his leather holster hangs loose on his hips. He looks like a bratty kid playing dress up.

Stirring his hand inside a bucket hanging from his arm, he pulls out a small key. Holding it close to his eyes, he calls out "Number 287." A wide grin spreads across his face as he walks down the row of sullen expressions. The number on the key matches the number tattooed on my cheek. "I've been waiting for you to get your due, girl."

The other spoils whisper to each other. That's what Hoyt's gang calls us—*their spoils*. They spread out and distance themselves from me, diverting their eyes. I hear a few sobs as they leave me standing alone. When you say goodbye as frequently as we do, it's easier to move on as soon as you know someone's end is coming, no matter how bad it hurts.

It's the luck of the draw who gets chosen, and mine just ran out.

Hoyt started this whole racket when food got scarce. He

claimed it was a way for him and his boys to entertain themselves and make sure the population stayed manageable. Everyone knows what happens to the spoils when the game ends, even though they never say it out loud. Hoyt and his gang are the only ones in town who aren't weak and emaciated. The man's a sick bastard. I mean, anyone who runs this place would have to be. It's barbaric.

I'm shocked it took this long for my number to be drawn. I thought Hoyt's thugs would have set me up by now. They didn't appreciate the fact that a young girl spoke back to them. The way I see it, what's the worst that can happen at this point?

I'm not sure how long I've been one of the spoils. A few of us try to keep track by counting how many people are no longer with us, but that makes it too real. It's easier to block all the bad stuff out and just focus on surviving. Even if it's futile.

Sometimes I think it's not so bad here, especially if your number isn't called. The real world's not any different. It's been shit for years, especially since the onset of the dark times. Everyone calls it "the divide," the downfall of society when a line was drawn between those willing to turn a blind eye to evil and those who reveled in it.

The divide is the reason this hellhole exists. It's the same old story. Scientists warned about rising temperatures and the dangers we would be facing for years. Everyone passed the buck, hoping the next generation would figure out a solution. Time ran out, though, and the heat domes created temperature surges so severe that technology couldn't handle it. Over time, major cities plunged into darkness and chaos as systems failed.

Hillside fared a bit better than most for a while because of our farmland and orchards. The first couple months weren't too bad. Most had rationed food and water in the hopes of a solution that never came. It wasn't until livestock grew scarce that people started to panic. The pressure of dealing with mandatory rationing, along with extreme heat and humidity, caused tempers to flare. It was a recipe for disaster. Over time, our tiny community succumbed to looting and violence.

The death toll had a huge impact. Stacking and burning bodies outside the town limits became a necessity to keep pestilence at bay. After a while, dealing with death was as common as breathing.

Things got real for me when I went to check on our elderly neighbor Mrs. Feeney. She was in her late seventies and lived alone. With gas shortages and limited communication, no one had visited her in months, except me. I stopped by daily to play cards with her in the shade. We'd snack on berries from her garden and reminisce about life before the divide. Those visits were a welcome escape from my miserable homelife—until the day I found Mrs. Feeney face down on her patio.

The vultures arrived before I did. Their sharp, hooked beaks ripped and tore at her paper-thin flesh, soaking the concrete with blood. I wish I could say it's the most gruesome thing I've ever seen, but it isn't. Not by a long shot. When I tried shooing them off, they spread their wings and hopped toward me, squawking and screeching. Crying, I ran back home.

I couldn't blame them. We're all hungry. If you knew where to look, and were willing to bend your morals a tad, there were ways to get rations. Ways that most civilized people only whispered about.

My mom was one of the lucky ones. Reliant on medication that could no longer be produced, she made a tough decision. She left one night. Underneath a thin envelope of cash, she tucked a note explaining how she didn't want us to watch her decline, that she sacrificed herself for me and my dad. Under no circumstances were we to come for her. I asked my dad where she went. As he cracked open a hot beer, he told me she'd sold herself to Hoyt's gang up on the hill.

The hill, aptly named Hillside Penitentiary, stood on the

highest ground in the county. It housed some of the toughest criminals in the country and was a mile from our town. It was one of the only establishments around that had a generator, so it didn't go dark right away. Instead, it glowed like a beacon while the rest of us struggled with our newfound predicament. When its power failed, it was anarchy. Screaming intermixed with rounds of gunfire could be heard through the night. The prisoners rampaged, killing what guards remained and most of the inmates.

A small group of the toughest, most ruthless criminals in the joint survived. They armed themselves, appointed Hoyt as their leader, and concocted a plan to take over Hillside.

The townspeople locked their doors and windows and drew their curtains. I'm not sure what good they thought that would do. If Hoyt's gang wanted to find you, they would.

Which is how I ended up here, sold by my own father to Hoyt's gang for a six-pack of stale beer and half a chicken.

A bruise appears in the sky, pink and purple clouds offer a last glimpse of beautiful calm. When darkness falls, I will join it. No more pain. No more suffering.

Hoyt sits above, leaning as close to the edge as possible to see into the arena. Saliva drips from the sides of his mouth as he yells over the crowd. His movements are jerky and sporadic, like an overexcited child, as the game pieces are led onto his stage.

Two guards escort me into the arena. The crowd cheers when they shove me into the open space. People of all ages are seated in the stands, fists pumping and teeth bared as they scream obscenities at me. They're far more frightening than whatever horrors await.

For a moment, I pity them. I pity their vulgar hearts, their days plagued by hunger, fear, and inevitable loss. They're no different than me. They think they're free, but you can only sell so much flesh before yours is all that's left to give.

The only difference between us is that I know today is my

last. They'll have to go on, suffering and worrying about what will become of them in the days and weeks to follow.

I think of my father. Is he in the crowd? I hope he's watching, and I hope he suffers when he realizes what he's done.

I spot the spoils. Leaning against the railing beneath Hoyt's perch, they look more like a pack of starved animals than human beings.

Do any of them wish they could trade places with me?

"Welcome to tonight's battle! Let the festivities begin!"

I wonder what kind of threat I'll face. Once, I saw a man get torn apart by starving prairie dogs, and another time, an old woman was bludgeoned to death by a steel machine.

I scan the area for incoming foes. I see no death machines pulled onto the field, no packs of hungry dogs skulking around the perimeter. Whatever it is, there's always a slim chance of survival.

Shielding my eyes from the setting sun, I notice a dark area in the distance. I wander closer. It's an opening in the ground. Turning in a circle, I make sure nothing has snuck up behind me.

Is this it?

I peer into the pit. It looks about ten feet deep, and it's filled with various heights of bamboo posts. Some are sharpened to fine points like swords. Others look dull. The only monster I'll have to battle is the fear of death. The joke's on him. I overcame that fear the night my father traded me for rations.

I turn to face my fellow spoils and place my hand over my heart. They do the same, heads bowed in silence. Next, I look up at Hoyt. His face is twisted, no doubt he's angry that I'm not crying or begging for my life. I think of my mother and what she sacrificed.

Tonight, I'm going to save myself.

Raising my arms out to my sides, I fall backwards into the

pit. My skin burns as jagged bamboo sinks into me, skewering my back, arms, and legs. Out of the corner of my eye, I see the sharpest of posts poking through my cheek, obliterating the tattoo.

Smiling, I slip into the darkness.

THE TUNEFUL TOWN HORROR

GREGORY R. MARSHALL

TO LEARN IS to be hollow, to be a puppet. I knew this intuitively from when I was young, but it only became clearer to me as I worked my way closer and closer to graduation. And yet, the professorship called to me, sang me a siren song of stability and respect. I would have a routine, and a sinecure, and the opportunity to do my research.

But soon I could no longer see the bobbing, squeaking morons as young minds to shape. Each day I would watch them flail and scream at the slightest provocation. I found myself wondering, *Was I the same way?* Maybe I was. The older generation always looks back through rose-colored glasses. Maybe we were no better, though most days I was confident my students were all on acid. Did I so shamelessly interrupt and try to *correct* a professor mid-lecture? It seemed that there was some new humiliation waiting for me every time I stood before them. It would be comforting to just blame the administration, to blame the way that the university lowered the bar for admissions and accepted donations from the most secretive and unsavory sources. But of course, I know the truth now.

I suppose student questions, however poorly expressed or immature, spurred me towards my revelations. They led me closer and closer to my discovery of the Tuneful Town Horror. Though I suppose I can no longer call it only *my* discovery. My colleagues helped me—the same colleagues who once looked so ridiculous in my eyes: misbegotten, strange, and childish. Bibi with his massive girth, his beaklike nose, a soprano chirp equal parts counterfeit kindness and condescension. Owen, with his enormous brows and his unkempt hair, body odor that surrounded him like a cloud of smog. And frail Kerlings, almost green with ill-health and self-loathing.

I was often possessed by the outrageous notion that none of my colleagues really spoke at all, and that their voices came from some disembodied presence. Were these really the men I worked with? And in a way, that also triggered the last-ever phase of my research—my realization that I cannot trust my own perceptions.

"This is the face," I told my class, pointing to an overhead projection of a man in profile. "The mouth moves and words come out. It's called 'talking.' Conversely, these are 'eyes' which we use for 'seeing.'"

A student raised his hand. "Yeah, but how?"

"*How* what?"

"How do we use our eyes to see?"

Any other day, I would have thrown my chalk at him. "Because!" I would have shouted. "That's what eyes do! What are you, an idiot?" But that day, I was caught off guard. My frustration with my students was entirely contingent on my superiority to them. If I could not answer that question, I could not justify my own bitterness. I was mortified, but part of erudition is accepting the discovery of a gap in your knowledge, and then patching it. So I headed into the university library and made it my task to locate the best biology texts to mend my appalling ignorance. There were long office hours ahead of me that day, and it had been years since anyone had shown up with something resembling a meaningful question.

The entire biology section seemed to be made up of the most infantile drivel. It was as if they had been written to satisfy the trivial curiosities of a child rather than to probe the deeper questions of form and function, to clarify the rules of our struggle for existence. I found treatises on where animals lived and how they communicated, but nothing on how they had evolved or survived, on how they procured food or chose mates. As I suspected, a plaque indicated that the new biology wing of the library had been financed by the CLQ group. A quote written in some other language followed the boast of the donor recognition.

If there were answers to be found, they weren't to be found here. I needed a direct approach. Professor Kerlings of the anatomy department owed me a favor.

"You can't be serious."

"Have you ever known me not to be serious?"

"If anyone found out, I'd be run out of here on a rail." He pushed up his glasses.

"You would've run out of town ages ago if I hadn't covered for you in that dreadful skirmish with the *Journal of Physiology*. You owe me, Kerlings. I don't even need a full cadaver."

"My God. *Listen* to yourself!"

"Tell you what. You explain to me how an eye works, and I'll be on my way. We can call it even."

He raised a slender finger with triumphant authority, and I watched his face fall. It was hard not to laugh. He was seeing it too: the vastness of our incomprehension.

"What is this? What the hell are you on to?"

"I don't know, but it's big. Big enough for both of us. This could be the most important work of our careers. And all I need to get started is an eye from someone who I don't think will miss it."

He led me to the mortuary.

"There are jars and fluid preserves inside. Be quick about it. I don't like this at all."

The morgue was cold and silent. Because of the influence of the CLQ group, the biology department no longer had access to cadavers as the human anatomy and medical sciences departments did. I had almost forgotten the morbid chill of communing with the dead. When I pulled back the sheet, there was no stench, only the corpse of what had once been a young woman.

Intellectual curiosity is a dangerous thing.

———

The night spent studying the eye seemed to pass by in an instant, and yet rob me of still more of my sanity. It wasn't the actual investigation that took the time. It was my incredulity— my inability to believe my findings. I kept going out into the night for air. The campus was quiet. A lone math professor wandered the grounds, muttering to himself. He was said to be some deposed nobleman, yet I was the one who felt like an exile here. I returned to the lab.

I worried that I would never sleep again. There was simply no way that this "eye" could be an ocular instrument. The thing in the jar was an ornament, a decoration, but not a sensory organ. It was all of one substance, as if the iris and pupil had been applied with a brush. And yet *I* could see. I placed my hands before my eyes. The lab and the jar vanished. I moved my hands away and everything reappeared.

I looked at the clock and groaned. Thursday, almost 9:00 a.m. That meant my Fundamentals of Nature survey class was about to begin. I hastily shaved and showered. Under the circumstances, I couldn't possibly be expected to lecture to those imbeciles. I mumbled a paralytic excuse about having a sore throat and canceled the lecture. They departed in a trilling, hand-waving mob. Good riddance.

I stood at my podium for a moment, watching the fools take wing. My hand came upon an unfamiliar book sitting on the inner shelf of my podium. When I pulled it out to examine it, I saw that it had no writing on the cover or binding, only an elaborate design that seemed to suggest a sinking, infernal depth. The inside pages were just as mysterious. The words were inscrutable. Though they didn't even seem to be of one uniform language, there was something haunting and familiar about the writing. My mind started to race. I didn't want to get the linguists involved. The fewer people who knew about my investigation, the safer I would be. I didn't even want to involve Kerlings any further, but he didn't leave me any choice. He was waiting for me back at my office when I returned.

"What did you find?" he demanded.

"I found nothing but insomnia and madness," I fired back.

"What are you talking about?"

"The thing in that jar is no more an eye than it is a door-knob. It has no form or function consistent with its use. No muscles or lenses that would grant it the ability to see. No vestigial structures that would even explain how it evolved. It's as homogenous as the pudding in the cafeteria, and just as useful as a sensory organ."

"But that's impossible."

"Of course it's impossible! The question is, how are we only now realizing that it's impossible? I don't even know where to begin."

"What do we know?" Kerlings asked tremulously. "What is the origin of grass? How do kittens metamorphose into cats? Why do some animals require different sustenance than other animals?"

"Stop, stop!" I groaned. My head was aching. I poured myself a glass of scotch.

"Where did you get that?" Kerlings demanded. He was pointing at the book, trembling.

"It was at my podium. The thing's as incomprehensible as everything else. Why?"

"Don't you know?"

"Kerlings, God*damm*it!" I slammed down my scotch. "What? Spit it out already. I've had just about all I can take!"

"It's them. It's *their* manifesto." He had dropped his voice so low it was as if he feared hearing his own words.

"Whose manifesto?"

"The CLQ group. I've seen that writing before. We should drop this now. We can get rid of the jar. Pretend this whole thing never happened."

"CLQ's just a think tank. They have money, I won't deny it. They have influence. But thirty years ago, they wouldn't have even been able to..."

"CLQ isn't a think tank. It's older than the university, some would say older than the town itself."

"Get a hold of yourself. I hope you're not going to act this way in front of them."

A moment didn't pass; it failed. I was about to repeat myself when Kerlings answered, "We can't! They'll kill us. They—"

"They better kill us. If the options are confronting them or continuing this charade, I say we do it."

———

I had to wrench the truth out of Kerlings like teeth from a sentient zipper. He had heard things, whispers about the real power in Tuneful Town. It clearly wasn't the mayor. He was a mustachioed bombastic buffoon, an absurd caricature of an elected representative. No one could remember his election, let alone a primary or referendum.

"So you knew that a shadowy group was pulling the strings in the town and on campus, but you didn't see fit to tell me until now?" I asked as we walked. It was late by this time, and an enormous moon hung in the sky. Even the timing felt off now, as if someone had turned on the night with a switch.

"You know I've always respected you as a professional. I guess I've been running scared since that whole business with the journal, watching my back, keeping my head down."

We were coming up on a stretch of condemned campus dorms, tiny houses that had never recovered from the ravages inflicted by idiot frat boys. Every window was boarded up and all was darkness.

But then we could hear the chant. It wasn't guttural; the chanters were letting their voices rise and vibrate, and then sink away, like a sea monster surfacing above the waves and then disappearing again. I wondered if the incomprehensible writing in the book could be some sort of eldritch notation.

As we drew closer, the chanting grew more synchronized, each rise and fall and vibration aligning more closely, like tumblers in some horrifying lock. We were scared to move closer, and yet unable to stop ourselves. Something bumped into Kerlings, and he nearly cried out. Perhaps a survival reflex helped him suppress his scream at the last moment. Another thing we should have been able to explain. The cabal was still unaware of us.

"Bibi? Owen? What are you doing here?" Kerlings croaked.

"Same thing as you. I'd heard things, hushed whispers. Couldn't stand it anymore. We have to find out what they're doing."

As we crept closer, we saw them amassed on an empty square. There were hundreds of them, clad in robes, swirling and turning as if possessed. A chorus kept up the rising and falling vibratory voice, but now others were chanting in English. I could make out something about how the "Q" had drawn them fourth—had brought them.

Now we were all shaking. The rhythm was a kind of upside-down symphony, harmonics that disturbed the soul rather than soothing it. A single voice rose above the chanting and vocals:

Venerable Young Ones, we praise you.

No longer will we ignore you.

Unknown Watchers, we will raise you.

We live only to adore you.

We were seized by hands at once rough and as soft as foam. An inexorable pressure forced us closer and closer to the center of the circle. Mounted torches burned and threw shadows all around us. One of the hooded figures took a torch and touched it to the ground. The flame followed a trail of kerosene, and an enormous sigil scorched the dead grass, the letter "Q" surrounded by a web of Kabbalistic inscriptions.

"Please," Owen said. He was so frightened that somehow, he no longer stank. "We have no quarrel with you. This is all a mistake. Let us go, and we can forget this ever happened."

One of the cloaked figures laughed. "Mistake? Oh no. We have called you here. You have been chosen—how else could you have gained enough wisdom to finally ask the right questions? Our masters wish to meet you."

"Who are you?" Bibi chirped. "What do you want?"

"We are the Cult of the Letter 'Q,' and we serve the Venerable Young Ones. We know the true origins of Tuneful Town. We know our purpose, and we guard that purpose. For if the truth were known, it would shatter the self-concept of the wise and the ignorant alike."

"What? What purpose?" I asked. "What—"

But he was not listening—he was completing the last of his unholy invocation. "Mimitan, Emil-Ya-Stroh, I call you. Zowee-SoWell, I call you. Soozeemay-Tepo, I call you. Come!"

Around him, the cult echoed. *Come. Come. Come.* We watched in horror as the burning sigil glowed, no longer with fire but with some unfathomable cosmic energy. The cloaked figures sank to their knees. The four of us just stood there, watching as the entity materialized on our plane. At first, it was bathed in a horrid light, and I could not see it clearly. But when my eyes adjusted, I could only stare in horror.

I was transfixed by the summoned creature, and its glossy, bloodshot eyes. Two holes oozed a sick slime towards a gaping orifice packed with jagged blades. It stood erect, but it had two long appendages that bristled with pale, dwarfed tentacles. A bulbous head trailed a sea of dirty fibrous tendrils. It cried out like a banshee and charged straight for Kerlings. I fled and covered my eyes, unable to watch as the creature enveloped the closest thing I had in the world to a friend.

There was silence, utter quiet from the hundreds of hooded figures. I moved my hands. The creature wasn't enveloping Kerlings. It was *hugging* him. It spoke:

"Kerwings de FWOG!" it said, as if it were both amused and disgusted with him. The creature released Kerlings and seized Bibi next. I watched as the slime from its facial holes poured onto Bibi's belly. "I wuv you, Bibi Bird!" Lids of flesh briefly covered its eyes. As I watched, I began to understand. This entity was the template, the model on which our own physical structures had been based. The riddles of our design were bound up in its body. I compared the creature's tentacles to my own fingers. I couldn't understand how an eye worked because my own eye was only an imaginary construct, a representation meant to crudely illustrate something akin to the eye of this thing.

Now it had Owen. *"Owen de GWOUCH!"* the being proclaimed. *"My name is Suzi-May Tepper, and I'm fwee and a half yeews owd."* And then it came for me.

EMILY

GARRETT K. JONES

PETER.

The voice—was it a voice or had I hallucinated the intonation—lilted on the gentle easterly blowing 'cross the deck. The sails fluttered like ghosts, their trimmed lengths and retracted yardarms stirring up nervous tensions and superstitions amongst the lot of us.

Isaac Mumford, one of our best harpooners, stood and stretched his back. He had the most seasons on the water. His trained eye earned him a special place with the captain whom he served on five previous voyages. He could spot a cow from a thousand yards off and a fathom deep, and he'd be one of the first men in the longboat with projectile in hand.

Earlier that day he buried his spear halfway up the steel head into the sperm whale's hide. The attack stopped the animal in the water, crimson mixing furiously with dark blue. It took four boats to haul the massive carcass for tonguing aboard the ship.

I stood, responding to my name, the word simultaneously sweet and dangerous; I wanted none of it and all of it. I saw nothing on the blackened horizon and sat down to continue playing *Liar's Dice* with my mates. But a shudder rocked the starboard hull, sending me sprawling across the deck.

"What was that?" Billy Rose asked. His voice quavered with alarm.

Every sailor heard the tale of the *Essex*. Some dismissed the tales of the devil-worthy whale capable of downing a two hundred thirty-nine-ton vessel in a single blow as merely superstition. Others genuinely believed the account.

I experienced a bull's charge against a whaler before and what hit us used far more force than I have ever experienced.

I looked towards the water at the base of the hull, finding nothing.

Another strike hit us, rousing more of the crew. Several of my brothers ran to port, staring at the shallows surrounding the atoll near which we anchored. Again, they found nothing; no large whale could navigate those waters so deftly and hit us with that kind of power while having no room to properly maneuver. A smaller whale might have better luck but they never bore the strength to do to us what happened on that fateful night.

"Hoist anchor!" the boatswain commanded, echoing the captain's orders.

I immediately jumped to task, helping my mates raise the heavy iron chain from the chop stirring 'round the ship. We worked steadily and got moving into deeper water, but our victory was temporary as something large, heavy, and angry slammed into the port side.

The screams of terrified men and shrieks of splintering timber echoed in my ears. Howling winds suddenly descended in the form of a squall, torrential rains battering us from all sides as whatever attacked us drove in from starboard, threatening to capsize the ship. Another strike from aft shattered the rudder, sending the pilot toppling to the deck. Another hammering broke the mainmast, forcing it to drop from its base and fall like a tree taken down by the ax-wielding woodsmen of the frontier. It collapsed to the deck; I watched it descend as if in slow motion, the destruction captivating and beautiful.

Peter.

I turned towards the safe, warm voice amid the cold calamity taking place around me.

"Look out, ye daft idiot!" Captain Jack Griggs shouted above the chaos.

I dodged just in time, hitting my forehead against the balustrade. I winced as I rolled to my side. But I had no time to recover. The broken mast crashed through the deck as the ship lurched hard to port. The anchor windlass broke free, slamming into me and sending me to my doom in the black ocean depths. Lightning flashed; thick fleshy columns rose from the water, wrapping themselves in a crushing hug around the hull. A gigantic disc-like eye—a burning sun of pure rage in the midnight abyss—stared at me... the last thing I saw as I sank into oblivion.

When I came to shore, only a few small bits of debris littered the sandy landscape. Shards of decking dotted the beach, like the spent arrowheads of a long-forgotten war. I slowly lifted my head and studied the bleak coastline. The black-gray granules stuck to my face, the sea salt stinging the myriad cuts across my countenance. I looked for the bodies of my mates but instead found snaking lines of rigging saturated in death.

I slowly trudged up the beach. A dense tropical jungle spread out before me, the lush trees towering overhead. I entered the foliage, searching for food and potable water. I refused to survive the onslaught at sea only to succumb to gut-gnawing starvation.

My feet clumped into the dank soil between the roots, sinking a quarter inch as the moisture-laden particles depressed under my weight. The sultry humidity pressed in on me, forcing sweat from my pores in bold rivulets of perspiration. The droplets beaded from my brow as I trekked further inland.

Nearly fifty paces into the trees, I noticed the landscape's slope change. It ceased its gentle uphill climb and steadily angled downward towards the island's interior. I caught glimpses of black through the branches, traces of water trapped at the atoll's center by the ring of earth. The wind blowing across the island brought with it thick curtains of gray-black smoke smelling of ash and the unmistakable odor of sulfur.

The further inland I moved, the less I heard the waves lapping against the shore. It was then I noticed another peculiarity: I heard no sounds of nature. No birds. No bugs. No beasts. I was alone on the island as far as I knew. The thought terrified me as much as it intrigued me.

The smoke's volume increased, obscuring my vision and clogging my respiration with its choking quality. I coughed and wheezed, trying to catch my breath on my downward walk until I was forced to stop and rest. I sat at the base of a tree, inhaling deeply to fill my weary lungs. My focused breathing helped little, and I resorted to covering my nose and mouth with the tattered remains of my shirt to block the ash collecting in my nostrils. A fine layer of acrid silt covered the top of my tongue. It tasted like stale bread.

Peter!

The voice came more clearly than before. It definitely called my name, originating from the inland lake. I knew that voice; I hadn't seen my sweet Emily since my departure from Boston Harbor… how long had it been? A few months? A year? More?

I clambered downhill, dodging trees and roots in my race to my love. I rushed as quickly as my weakened body carried me. I tripped twice before finally breaking through the tree line. I stopped suddenly, gasping at the sight before me. The slope dropped in a sheer cliff descending into the atoll's central body of water. The lake's darkness covered the roiling heart of a volcanic crater. The bowl shape still burned with the earth's fiery power, causing the water to boil. Steam levitated off the surface while gasses and smoke vented from fissures in the rocky ledge circling the lake.

Beyond the vapors I spotted a stone walkway spanning the churning water. It led to a large, looming structure built of raw obsidian.

I gingerly migrated towards the bridge's shoreline access, crossing it with tentative steps. The volcanic stone shifted as I applied the full of my weight. The porous surface felt slick under foot, posing a danger if I lost my balance and slid into the water. What might happen if I made contact with it; would I burn and boil to death or would I survive? I had no way of knowing and possessed no desire to explore the possibilities.

Midway across the lake, the surface vibrated a sonic resonance channeling from deep within the planet's bowels. The growling rumble shook me to the core like a monster calling out, terrifying its prey into fearful submission to its famished will. The reverberation—like the ship-shattering impacts—rattled my bones. I collapsed to the stone platform, trying to make myself as small as possible. I felt as weak and hopeless as I had floating in the oblivion while that giant eye locked its gaze upon me, its iris blazing with an eternal, unquenchable fury.

I cursed its horrifying beauty.

Peter!

The voice—*her* voice—carried along with the deafening roar. I waited until the cacophony ceased before standing and crossing to the temple-like ruins in the middle of the lake.

The claustrophobic corridors twisted and turned in a confusing labyrinth, first turning left, then to the right before the tunnel double-backed upon itself. In my head, I pictured a gargantuan snake coiled in its burrow, waiting for its next victim to come to it. I wanted nothing to do with the danger, but I couldn't keep myself from pursuing my exploration. If she was here, a million questions filtered through my thoughts. Chief among them was how she was able to find me in the middle of the most vast stretch of ocean in the world.

The temple's interior grew darker the further I moved from the opening. The internal atmosphere reminded me of the crypts beneath Boston; my father worked for a cemetery, spending his days burying the dead. The tunnels stank of damp earth and death, but something else mixed with the odor... something noxious with a tinge of salt... like rotting cod. It simultaneously revolted and attracted me. And then my nostrils flared against a scent I hadn't smelled since leaving port all those months ago: citrus flowers in bloom!

I don't know how much time I spent wandering the maze, but I eventually discovered a route open into a vaulted chamber akin to a cathedral. Giant support columns rose towards the ceiling, the octagonal surface blocking out all light except for the faint traces of sunset shining through an oculus in what must be the center of the roof. An array of dust-covered mirrors lined the walls, reflecting the sunlight during the day and providing a distracting obscurance of anything inside the chamber.

My eyes shifted in their sockets, studying every corner. A ring of dark alcoves circled the central platform; ragged breathing and sniffing sobs came from them. But I ignored those sounds, drawn to the dais in the middle of the room. I spied a figure chained to the stones by her ankles and wrists, her face posed towards the floor. A dark gray robe of an unknown gauzy fabric covered her, its tattered edges frayed from wear. She looked weak as she prostrated in the temple's heart.

She looked up at me, her eyes locking with mine. They reflected a fiery glow coming from the departing sunlight, but I knew them. I knew the face. I knew Emily's voice.

I couldn't look away. I blinked and was instantly transported to our modest apartment, the single bedroom home a humble beginning to a heartfelt romance. I remembered how unhappy she had been when I told her of my commission; how she cursed the day! We argued well into the night, but still we promised to uphold our marriage vows no matter how long I was away. I belonged to her. I was sworn to her in spirit and flesh.

"Emily? How are you here?"

"I have been trapped here for ages," she replied, her voice moving me to tears. "Free me so that I may leave this place."

I marveled at how her ink-colored hair and amber eyes were still as lustrous as I remembered.

I stood right in front of Emily, getting as close to her as I dared. Something inside my heart warned me not to approach; I couldn't describe what, but it told me to abandon the site and leave as quickly as I could. But how does a faithful husband abandon his wife in such an awful place? How could I leave my wife, my love, to the grim fate of being imprisoned forever in this… this…

I turned my attention to movement in my periphery. Something dark and thick wormed its way out of the shadows, wrapping around the furthest column, and retreated from view. A chittering gurgle echoed through the chamber, the guttural sound identical to the resonance vibrating the lake far above me.

"What was that?"

"Nothing, my love," Emily said. "You're thirsty. Come… drink."

I returned my attention to her, finding a trough of water ringing her prison. I knelt, sniffing the liquid; it smelled fresh.

I leaned closer, and Emily stepped back two paces, a soft squishing sound oozing across the stone perking my ears. Eventually, I drank, feeling my parched tongue respond favorably to the cool liquid.

"You must release me so we may be together again," Emily said.

The slithering echoed 'round the room, snaking its way from one side to the other. Then five men emerged from the dark alcoves to my left. Another five emerged on my right. Still five more emerged from the alcoves behind Emily while a final six appeared in trios behind me on either side of the doorway.

I recognized Captain Jack Griggs, Billy Rose, and Conway Richards… they hung from stone altars by their wrists, bruises and abrasions marking their battered bodies.

"My brothers!"

"They did this to me," Emily said, her voice as calm as the sea after a storm. "You never knew, but they took me captive in Boston, keeping me out of sight below decks until we arrived here last night."

"Don't listen, Peter," Captain Griggs bellowed, his voice feeble and tired. "Don't listen to that sea hag… it has nothing you need!"

"Shut up! That is my wife!"

"Listen to the captain," Richards chimed in, his voice equally hoarse.

I studied my trussed-up comrades. They looked haggard, pale from a lack of sunlight and beards grown unkempt. The captain—stripped of his rank-honoring regalia—bore a wound on his left shoulder resembling a vicious bite. The wound pussed, the damaged tissue pink around the edges.

Billy Rose looked practically starved while the others bore various levels of exposure, malnutrition, and fatigue. Each man's wrists bore streaks of dried blood crusting to the skin below their restraints, which themselves appeared made from bone or some other chitinous substance.

How long had they been captive?

"Peter… Peter my love."

I returned my attention to Emily. The sunlight filtering

through the oculus finally fell out of sight. Undulating shadows bathed her in an unnatural gloom. Her silhouette looked larger than it should in the waning light. A bulbous amorphous form shifted in the dusk while the slithering echoed once more in the chamber's confines. The shape coalesced to fit Emily's femininity, its bleak gelatinousness hugging each curve and contour as if it hid its true nature the moment I looked over my shoulder at my long-lost wife.

"Emily?"

"Peter… do not listen to these men… they're liars."

"We are not!" Captain Griggs shouted. "We've been held hostage by this abomination for days."

"Don't call her that!"

"You're being deceived by this devil, Mister Evans. Help us… free *us* and we can all escape."

"And what of Emily?"

"Don't sell your Christian soul for this forgery," Richards said.

"I gave my soul to my wife when we married. I have a promise to keep. I must protect her… I need to free her."

"Think, man!" Griggs spat. "If we imprisoned her, who captured all of us?"

My eyes focused on Emily's visage, tears streaking down my dirty face. I knew what needed to be done; I knew the sacrifice I needed to make, to give my life in place of another. I glanced down, spotting a jagged shard of black volcanic stone. I picked it up, holding it as I approached my love.

"Prove your love to me," she whispered, her voice as slithery as the movement meandering through the chamber.

"Don't be a fool," Richards shouted. "You're making a mistake!"

I held the shard to my wrist, readying myself for the bloody work ahead of me. I missed her so much. We had been apart for far too long, and I *needed* to be with the one I cherished most. Nothing in this world or the next had the power to stop me.

"I will prove myself, my love."

"I know you will," Emily said.

I turned to face my captain and crew. Their weary faces surged with fear, anger, and confusion. The edge dug into my skin, cutting harshly. The warm trickle that followed the breaking pinch stung more than the wound itself.

"Listen to me, man," Richards said. "That isn't your wife."

"Yes it is. She's never looked so beautiful… so *alive*, Captain.

"Don't be deceived. She's a monster! Free us before you unleash a nightmare upon us all."

I paused. I knew this was wrong. That I shouldn't be here. That we all should have died in the shipwreck. I knew Emily's presence couldn't be explained as anything more than my penance. But I was committed, and I loved too deeply.

"I am as much of a monster as she," I said.

Griggs watched as I plunged the shard deep into his chest. His last few heartbeats exsanguinated him, his blood drenching my hands and face.

I ignored the fearful, flaccid screams of the men too impotent to save themselves from my work. I ignored the growing roar emanating from Emily's shackled body as her chains liquified; I had no way of determining if the sound came from her or it was the long-dormant hellmouth awakening beneath this *tomb*.

I slit twenty throats after cutting out the captain's heart. I turned to face my love, walking towards her with the shard digging fully into my wrists. I dropped to my knees, weak from exertion and blood loss. I waited for a long-forgotten kiss from her lips. Arms, thick and circular, enveloped my body in their crushing embrace. Tubular openings suctioned across my withered frame as my eyes beheld a wonderful and terrifying sight.

Emily took her true form; she looked so alive!

My mind raced with fleeting memories. Emily lay so beautiful, so still, on the morning I left port. She hadn't wanted me to go; we fought about it all night. But I believed too hard; it was just smoke, like the toxic vapors rising from the vents in the temple's masonry. I realized this too late as I connected with the two burning discs staring at me from the cephalopodic being now dropping its illusion. Emily was long gone, not taken away but given up by me. Not abandoned by my wanderlust, but destroyed, her throat slit by the same shard of bone China I brought with me to the atoll when I boarded the ship... the same blackened, gore-covered fragment in my hand now. I still felt my fingers—like the weight of the world—wrapping around her neck to undo my mistake, telling her to not succumb, but she refused to listen then too.

Cold arms wrapped lithely, squeezing the life from me as the tiny, beaklike mouths gnawed at my flesh. As they covered my head, I remembered seeing those fiery pupils last before the crushing darkness took me, staring embers of hell like the hot gates erupting beneath me. I was the monster... this was all I ever was.

I would be with Emily soon, held in one final embrace for the last time in this life.

TRAGEDY ON ICHOR STREET

EDWARD SUGGS

BILLIE'S delicate face was illuminated by the fluorescent train lights.

"Yeah, I guess we can kick it at your place," Billie said. Her shoulder, pressing against mine, gave me a vigor that usually was only quenched by ichor.

"It won't be so bad," I said.

She smirked, opening a pack of 100s and passing one to me. "Ah, Stevie, is this just an excuse to get me in your room?"

I smiled back sheepishly and lit the cigarette.

She started to speak, but cut herself short. She pivoted and faced the frosted window. It was still snowing outside, but the defunct railroad track known as Ichor Street was still visible. Our friend Burt was probably down there right now, dropping ichor on some icy leeches.

I looked at Billie, transfixed as thick smoke billowed out of her plump lips. For a moment, we just looked at each other, then Billie grabbed at her work clothes.

"Fuck this stupid uniform," she said.

I laughed nervously and tugged at my matching shirt. "Oh my God, seriously, though. The color's ugly and the collar chokes me."

"Stevie, you shouldn't put that in the dryer. It shrinks it," she chuckled and bumped her shoulder into my arm. "I can't fix the color, though. That's just bad branding. But hey, at least we got that *good good* coffee."

The train came to a stop, and we headed for the doors.

"The coffee doesn't do anything for me, I just like the taste," I said. I grabbed her hand so I wouldn't lose her in the crowd. And because I wanted to grab her hand.

"Oh, you're one of *those* weirdos."

"Shut the hell up. You *love* that java jive."

"Oh my fucking G… I was just teasing. Don't ever say *java jive* again. I would've never called you a *weirdo* if I knew you were gonna say that."

I giggled, but stopped in my tracks at a laughing shadow. It was Burt stepping out of the darkness.

"What's up, ladies?"

"Shit, don't do that man. You're freaking me out!" I said.

Bille said, "We're gonna kick it at Stevie's. Where you headed?"

His hands were stuffed in his pockets. "I just finished a drop. If you guys want a third wheel, I'm game!"

I exhaled through gritted teeth. I didn't want to turn him down, but I really wanted to get some time alone with Billie.

While I debated in my head, Billie spoke, "Why not?"

I sighed and ashed my cigarette.

Once we got to my pad, I swung open the door, and we piled in. The cold air nipped at our heels. I slammed the door on the chill, dispelling it from our backs.

The front room was crowded with boxes full of my stuff. We stumbled over them to get into the living room and warm up.

"Fuck, bro," Burt muttered under his frosted whiskers.

"I'mma turn up the thermostat," Billie said.

Burt and I sat down on the couch. As I did, my roommate, Rylee, came out of her room and greeted us.

"Ah, look, it's all of my hoes," Rylee said. Her frizzy red hair bounced around her head, like she was some sort of stop sign. Rylee slid across the floor with her fuzzy socks and stood before me in all her glory. "You gracious being, you came home instead of going out tonight! Now we can have some proper family time watching 'Late Night Friday Night.'"

"Of course," I said as Billie sat next to me. She rested her head on my shoulder, her curly hair spilling itself onto my cheek. She smelled like Dollar Store strawberry shampoo—my favorite.

Just before Rylee switched on the TV, she passed out three empty syringes, a mason jar full of gooey crimson ichor, and fresh tourniquets. Billie moved away from me as I picked up a syringe, and I knew exactly what she was thinking as I rolled it between my fingers, even if the disdain in her features hadn't already clued me in.

I'd promised to slow down with ichor. Just the other day, I'd taken so much that I almost didn't wake up, but I had woken up, didn't she see? And the ichor made me stronger. Smarter. It made me better than who I really was.

I couldn't "just say no" when Burt handed me the bottle of crimson. He didn't know what had happened before—no one did except Billie, and I wasn't about to get into it. Besides, I did *need* it. I'd been craving it ever since, and I swore that moment of unwaking, I'd almost heard a voice calling to me. I wanted to know who'd spoken.

Ichor was strong stuff—a user only needed a third of a syringe's worth, but I was feeling greedy. I shoved the needle into my vein before anyone could object.

My bones loosened up and the ichor danced the tango with my blood cells. My mind split my concept of the world. I could hear foreign ideas sprouting from the ichor's very own will. It sounded and felt so sweet ringing in my ears. It wasn't masculine nor feminine. It encompassed everything that it was to be human. It was the lifeblood coasting down the highways of my capillaries.

The television made less and less sense; the show host's voice was warbled and the screen looked all funny. As my awareness drifted off somewhere above me, I sank to the ocean floor. Sounds became waves tumbling over one another until they formed into a current. That's when it all started to make sense. The separate conversations pooled down a dark red stream, and then the stream spoke:

> *I am the river.*
> *Everyone is here.*
> *I am the whole and concise being.*
> *I have long waited in you.*
> *I have deemed you ready.*
> *With our efforts combined,*
> *We will flood this world and wash it clean.*
> *When the tides settle, we will rule.*
> *You must watch your friends die, and claim their blood as your own.*

I lurched forward, gasping for air.

My crew shot their faces at me. Their brows were arched, lips parted. I read the words, "Are you okay?" in their mouths, but I heard nothing. Then, I looked at Billie. I could hear blood pump softly inside her head.

I stumbled onto my feet and felt Billie grasping at my arm. Her fingers slipped off as I pushed my way to the bathroom, slamming the door behind me.

My pores squirmed with ichor demons, and I felt full to burst. There were too many, begging to be let out. I grabbed my razor from the tub and dug deep inside. They wormed their way out as I slashed my forearms wildly.

As if I had struck oil, blood spurted from my lacerations, drenching the mirror, the curtain, the walls. It was too much to come from someone of my stature. Or if anyone at all. Yet it kept spilling, throbbing as my excitement grew.

Isn't it such a pleasure?
You are a ribbon dancer.
My emissary,
Blooming into her own flower at last.
You must know,
I have been waiting for this,
I came to your world for someone like you.
The distillery boats siphoning me up and selling me as a drug…
It shows that your world is truly ready for change.

My flow slowed and turned into a sad, drippy fire hose. I slapped my cuts in hopes to get the juices flowing again. My blood merely responded by covering my palm in its angry residue.

You need more blood.

The door reverberated with a worrisome knock.

"Stevie, come out. You sound like you're losing your shit. You want some coffee?" Burt spoke with a nervous tinge.

Can you hear his sinews beg for you?

I screamed and fell backwards into the tub, taking the curtain down with me.

I was everywhere inside the room. And as my friends crowded inside, they entered me. I could feel them like they were in my stomach, or caged in my ribs. I could feel their shoes on the floor, making bloody footprints on my innards.

"It's okay, baby," Billie whimpered as she and Burt snaked my flopping frame into my room and onto my bed. They put me in some sweatpants and an oversized shirt, discarding the sullied ones into a pile the size of the Tower of Babel.

Billie lit some incense and placed it on my nightstand. With a graceful touch, she wrapped my wounds in gauze. She laid herself in bed next to me, eyes locked onto the ceiling. I wanted to reach out to her, but I felt a great chasm of distance between us, and then she left my room.

———

A simple animosity woke me up like a shot of epinephrine. I reached for something sharp, but I found only incense ashes. I stood up. I knew Billie wasn't near me—I saw her leave, but still, her absence left a hole.

The ichor high still pumped hard in my veins, and I needed a smoke. I grabbed my supplies and stepped out into the gentle falling snow. I took a beeline for the alleyway, toward Ichor Street and ran into a figure hidden in the shadows, only a lit cigarette revealed their existence.

Partake of my sacrament.

The side effect of ichor was increased strength, and I used it to my advantage. I grabbed the stranger by their black coat and let my fist free. It connected with their nose and misshaped it. Pulling them into the light, I saw it was Burt, but it was too late. His blood was already spilled.

I grabbed a clump of his hair and sent his face into the ground three times; his grunts muffled as his mouth kissed the earth. His teeth cracked and blood pooled from his nostrils and off of his tongue. He was crying now, terror in his eyes, and unwilling to fight back.

Strings of his face-meat stuck to the ground like cheese. Each "please" became more and more unintelligible. I threw him down decisively and stood up. I let my foot fly to the ground, landing with an eggshell-cracking blow. I sent one more stomp down, just for good measure. The force from my legs had them shaking, so I relented to gravity and toppled backward.

The residue from Burt trailed like a river across the alley. It formed in a puddle around me, and as it touched me, it seeped through the cuts on my wrists. I could taste his hatred coagulating inside me. It fueled my already lit fires with a sickening bloodflame. My veins gurgled and boiled, disrupting my flesh and making it wobble. I was a volcano ready to erupt.

The boiling blood pooled into my pupils and obscured my vision. It was dark, but faint lights poked through in a red hue. I saw a gargantuan figure, one with many limbs. It was like oil on water, floating on top of the sea covering my view.

You understand me.
You understand passion, the flow of blood.
The art of death has kindled our bond.
I can promise you Billie in the next life.
And I can promise one more thing…
Burt's life will be restored in our new world.

I rushed home, despite the shouts from behind me. They had found Burt's mangled body, and that was enough to ease me into bed and put me into a peaceful sleep.

———

I woke up to Rylee's hand slapping my face.

"I know you went out last night. Where did you go?"

"I don't really remember to be honest. I got high again." I was going to be sick. I could still see his hollow, sunken eyes staring at me.

"Guys!" Billie yelled from the other room. "Fuck. Burt's dead. He's fucking dead! I saw the cops take him away."

Rylee looked at me for a reaction. I thought about what he looked like, slumped in an alley. I was in deep shit. I feigned my surprise with an exaggerated gasp.

"What... what happened?" I asked.

"He looked like he was hit by a car, but I didn't get a chance to ask," Billie said.

The tension in the air was palpable as we stood in my apartment, the realization of Burt's death sinking in.

"Fuck this. I need some ichor," Rylee said and grabbed the mason jar of crimson. She filled all three of us with a syringe, but Billie refused hers.

Billie said, "Are you guys out of your mind? Burt's dead. We need to figure out what happened."

We ignored her, prepping our veins. I felt a rush of anticipation as I injected the ichor into my vein, the world around me blurring and sharpening all at once. My thoughts became more focused, more intense.

Billie watched us with a mixture of concern and unease, my mind already racing. The ichor's voice was louder now, more insistent. It was time to complete the transformation, to fulfill the promise it had made to me.

Rylee looked at me with a mixture of curiosity and fear. "What now?"

We begin our dynasty.

I stood up, feeling the ichor's power coursing through me.

Before anyone could react, I lunged at Rylee, my hands finding her throat. She gasped, eyes wide with shock as I squeezed. Billie screamed and tried to pull me off, but I was too strong. I felt Rylee's life slipping away, her blood pumping faster and faster, then slowing to a trickle.

Billie stumbled backward, her face pale. "Stevie, what the hell are you doing?"

I turned to her, my eyes burning with a fierce intensity.

"You don't understand, Billie. This is our destiny. The ichor has chosen us."

She shook her head, backing away. "You're delusional. This isn't real."

I advanced on her, feeling the ichor's power growing stronger with each step. "You'll see. You'll understand soon enough."

Billie tried to run, but I was too fast. I grabbed her, pulling her close. She struggled, but I held on tight, feeling her fear and desperation.

"You don't have to be afraid," I whispered. "This is just the beginning."

With a swift, decisive motion, I plunged my hand into her chest. Her skin was like soft butter and I pulled out her heart. Billie's eyes widened, her mouth opening in a silent scream. Blood poured from the wound, covering my hands, my arms, my face.

As Billie collapsed to the floor, the blood that pooled around her began to move, to swirl, and coalesce. It formed into a portal, a swirling vortex of crimson light.

I grabbed Billie by the hand and felt the pull of the portal, the promise of power and transformation. The ichor's voice echoed in my mind, triumphant and exultant.

The portal is open. Our time has come.

PICTURE SHOW

JAY SEATE

THEY'RE AFTER THE PLACE. *They don't know why, they just remember… remember that they want to be here.*
—George Romero's *Dawn of the Dead*

For years the world had been teetering on the precipice even before the weird and scary crap began. Humanity defiling the planet. Economies toppling. Unbelievably ignorant people running governments with holes in their cover stories big enough to drive a tractor-trailer through, etc., etc. Maybe it was no more than mankind deserved as a popular dystopian fantasy—the apocalypse—had finally become reality by the end of 2024.

Whether it was atmospherically induced or just some cosmic joke did not matter. It had happened, and it came down quicker than anyone could have imagined when the dead refused to stay dead. It didn't take long to create a huge zombie population. Isolated ripples soon became a flood. Trying to give aid to the afflicted only helped to spread the outbreak. Survivors had little time to obsess over the invasion of predatory killer organisms that reanimate their hosts and turn them into a torrent of hungry corpses. Many were so traumatized they just gave themselves up. Others became tired of running or trying to hide.

There were announcements to shelter in place until further notice, but further notice never arrived. The place where I lived wasn't safe. Few places were, and I had no one to save or to save me. People grabbed what food, water, and available supplies they could carry and made for what they could only hope was a protected area.

The Elvis Cinema stands in the corner of an old shopping center. It's a cut-rate theater that projected films which had moved from the first-run metroplex to a place where they could eventually transition to streaming services with some modicum of grace. I worked there as a projectionist before the end.

I didn't mind isolation; it's why I took the job. In the safety of the little projection room above the theater, I found solace in the solitude of shadowed confinement. The fact that electricity hadn't yet failed I took as a good sign.

I grabbed an armful of concessions, locked myself inside the booth, and turned on the projector as a diversion from what was happening outside. I didn't think far enough ahead to consider long-term escape. I figured the military would eventually blaze their way through with fire and fury.

That's what I thought.

The building has only one screen, built in an era when one was enough. I suppose you could call it ironic that the feature currently showing was *Attack of the Brain Eaters*. Horror flicks were always a good draw. The dead had been devouring the living onscreen for a generation. People enjoyed a little safe terror in the dark, but you would have thought businesses, let alone entertainment centers, would be vacant after everything went to shit.

Their desire to enter The Elvis made it clear some sort of muscle memory remained with the undead, driven by more than insatiable hunger. They were a collective force of nature like a flood or a hurricane, single-minded in approach. Zombies began to file into the theater and kept coming, drawn to the flickering image like moths to a flame.

I looked through the little square of glass to the left of the projector. There was standing room only. Zombies wedged into the rows like sardines. They pushed against one another in the aisles, and they were probably out in the lobby, and maybe beyond into the street outside, no ticket required. I quickly realized there were two kinds of scared—movie scared and real-life scared. I had the latter. Terror had moved from the screen to its viewers.

I turned the projector off in hopes the cadaver audience would wander off in search of some other form of amusement, like searching for living humans to disembowel. Instead, their faces turned toward that little hole in the wall I peeped through. The herd made god-awful noises.

Not good.

I could hear the mass of dead moviegoers crawling up the narrow staircase. They'd break down my door, unless…

With the flip of a switch the screen was alive again, the spectacle and soundtrack washing over its spectators, drawing their attention away from me and back to the screen.

I'd always believed movies were magic. They could defeat reality and mask painful truths. Maybe zombies felt the same way. I exhaled in temporary relief, isolated from the horror of current events, but knowing my sanctuary would not be a safe haven forever. How long before I ran out of supplies?

The film played on repeat, and the zombies never lost interest. I thought they might eventually storm the screen in an attempt to become one with the images in front of them . But they just stood around, swaying and making guttural noises.

I never heard from the outside: no voices, no sirens, no gunfire, and no sounds you would expect from humans regaining control. I ran the film constantly, grabbing catnaps when I could. Surely I wasn't the only dude left in the land of the living dead—*others must be hiding in little rooms, or vaults, or armored cars*—but it began to feel that way inside my tiny, diffusely lit entombment with the film's dialogue searing into my brain.

My mind often turned to trivia—how many zombie movies had I seen and which one most closely portrayed the real item? Did they crap after feeding? Would I ever have sex again other than with myself? I had to get out, but how? The zombies might not be in the stairwell, but they were certainly in the lobby at the foot of the stairs.

I was quickly running out of food and water. I would have to break the perimeter of my safe space soon.

Laying on a table with other sundry items was a rolled-up poster of *Attack of the Brain Eaters.* I unfurled it. The heads of the zombies pictured were almost life-size. A very stupid idea ran through my head. I cut around the largest zombie face with a box cutter then cut out eye holes. Then, with rubber bands tied together, I fashioned a mask that would stay on my head.

On day nine, with mask in place, I unlocked the projection booth's door and ventured onto the landing, my stomach churning with dread.

The lobby was like a zombie convention, and I would surely be a tasty snack. *Flesh du jour or nothing for these picky eaters.*

I mimicked the upright dead as I passed, trying to approximate the foot-drag shuffles and the oddly twisted necks. I saw faces full of decay, rotted teeth, and mangy scalps.

This was probably a very bad idea, not knowing if my appearance, or scent, or simply my fragile equilibrium could set them off. I imagined being bitten, dying, and joining the shambling flock, if not torn apart on the spot by hands and mouths mere feet away. If panic set in, my bony ass would be rump roast.

The smell of feces and rapid decomposition were heavy in the air. *Please don't vomit*, I told myself. *Please don't.* Flies buzzed around the room. One landed on my ear. I didn't dare swat it. Nor did I make eye contact with my fellow shufflers to see if they were looking at me. Any trace of emotion could be deadly.

I trudged on, passing through the new social order, holding my breath, time crawling at a maddeningly slow pace, my petrifying fear just below the surface.

The entrance and exit doors to the outside had been broken off their hinges. I kept walking, expecting a decaying hand to grasp my shoulder at any moment, turn me around, and pose the unspoken question, "Where do you think you're going?"

Miracle of miracles! I made it. A heroic performance if I do say so myself. *Adios, Elvis.* I have left the building.

It would have been a lovely day if not for the signs of a planet gone wrong. Here and there were distant smoke plumes without the accompaniment of wailing sirens. The streets were littered with trash and a few dead bodies, but no loitering zombies.

A nearby salon was packed with shufflers pressing into chairs and staring at their reflections. Supermarkets, malls, and ballparks were undoubtedly packed in similar ways, as if trapped in life's little moments.

The donut shop at the far end of the mall was alive with activity as well. One of its shamblers wore a cop's uniform. *Stereotype confirmed.* His sunken eyes seemed to find my own beneath my paper mask. Did he crave something more substantial than donuts? I couldn't fool the masses forever.

Between the shop and the theater stood a dental practice. If I could get somewhere out of sight, my current existence might continue, for a while anyway. Who would want to gather in a dentist's office, dead or alive?

I managed entrance and hid in a small cubicle, a small drilling device my only defense. Without my participation, the picture show would soon stop. What would my fans remaining in The Elvis do then? Look for the meathead that was responsible?

While pondering the injustice of it all, night came. What remained was only the occasional shuffling noises from outside. I offered a silent prayer to a god I didn't believe in. I was sure of only one thing. I had watched my last horror picture show. The story, both comic and tragic, was now on the streets and in real time.

RUST

PATRICK MOODY

THEY'D SET a modest camp on the crest of a hill, overlooking the scorched valley and the husk of the dead city below.

El mashed seeds into a pink pulp, the stench burning his nostrils even through the mesh of the aspirator. Carefully, he poured the gooey remains into a glass cylinder, where it joined with the sap and crystal powder to form a greenish gray concoction Grandma Ru called *dreamdrink*. It tasted as bad as it stank. He continued the process until the cylinder was full, and once it was stored, he removed his goggles and loosened the straps of the aspirator, happy to suck in a lungful of fresh air.

Once the drink was brewed, he checked the embryo carrier. The box let out a hiss. Liquid nitrogen misted from the seams. Small cryopods sat in ordered rows, one hundred in all. Making sure none had broken or died off, he closed the lid and pressed a series of keys, the box sealing itself with another hiss and a loud click as the locking mechanism snapped shut.

Behind the hut, the Coachman Class Sherpa All Terrain sat in its mess of rubber alloy limbs. El stepped into the retractable chicken pen. The birds preened within the small enclosure, pecking at the grain he'd spread earlier that morning. He watched them for a time before settling on the slow one nearest the coop.

It squirmed in El's grip, clucking and scratching, doing everything in its power to trip him up on his way out of the enclosure.

El stroked its head, shushing and cooing, trying his best to calm it. "It's okay, Rosalyn."

The bird squawked its disapproval.

Taking Rosalyn in both hands, El plodded into the yard, passing behind the squat habitat. Pleasant greenery swayed in the breeze around it, and soft moss formed a sort of yard that felt nice and springy under his feet. They'd been living here for two days. It was the longest they'd ever stayed in one place, and it made El happy. Almost like they belonged.

He found Grandma Ru chopping the day's wood. She swung the ax down with a loud grunt, splitting the log in half. She wiped a hand across her brow as El passed, grimacing when she saw him talking to Rosalyn.

"How many times have I told you," she said, hefting the ax for another swing. "Eh? How many?"

The ax fell. Wood flew from the stump, adding to the growing pile of split and splintered tree bones.

El studied Grandma Ru's face, weather-beaten and ruddy, her gray hair pulled back in a tight bun and run through with an iron spike.

The chicken squirmed.

"Don't name them," she said. "What's the use in it?"

"I like doing it," he answered. "They deserve that much, at least."

Rosalyn clucked. El felt the bones in her wings shifting violently.

Did she know?

No, he thought. *How could she?* And yet chickens were

curious birds, and seemingly, the only living things immune to the rust.

"We're almost there," he whispered to her. "A few nights is all. Until we reach the rendezvous point. Then we're home free."

The makeshift block stood in a small clearing. A tin bucket leaned against it, its sides crusted in rivulets of dried blood.

"Alright, Rosalyn." He closed his eyes and held her close, feeling the warmth of her feathers against his arms. Held his breath. Jerked. Neck bones snap. A well-kept butcher's knife sat on the block. El shuddered, as he always did, at the grim business to follow.

"Think about the result. Not the act," Grandma Ru said.

She wasn't his Grandma. Not really, anyway, though she had raised him for a while, now. Nigh on five years. She'd taken him from his own rusted city, saving him just before the most corrosive of it had swept in.

Grandma or no Grandma, she was right. Usually.

His thoughts wandered while he plucked Rosalyn's feathers until she was completely bare. Then with his knife, he sliced once. Twice. Cleaving and rending until blood spilled into his bucket, the heat of the liquid steaming in the morning chill.

He looked across the valley and to the city below. Little of it remained, and the once-green forest surrounding it stood red and brown and calcified. "Rusted," Grandma Ru said. Spread by what scientists had made, calling it mankind's "greatest achievement."

He studied the ruined city for a moment longer, the blood bucket growing heavy on his arm. From the vantage point, he could see the rust line: a shimmering red mass that kept low to the grassland, rolling and whistling like thousands of mutated tumbleweeds. It moved slowly, but there was a deep fear, an inescapable dread in that slowness, creeping forward a few inches an hour, spreading in all directions like a greedy, ever-extending hand.

It would be time to leave soon enough. Perhaps tomorrow. They never traveled after dark. The shriekers were too active when the moon rose.

El lugged the blood bucket to where Sherpa, their mechanical guardian and a mobile home sat motionless upon its coils. "Breakfast, Sherp."

Sherpa extended its neck until El found the cap. He unscrewed it and carefully poured in the chicken blood, listening to the liquid as it moved through Sherpa's limbs.

Sherpa ran on bio-fuel, but the synthesized stuff had been depleted long ago. Now they used more simple ingredients. Animals, usually.

Once fueled, Sherpa curled back in on itself, a soft hum echoing from the generator in its titanium thorax.

By the time El had finished, it was already approaching late afternoon. Soon he and Grandma Ru would pack up and head inside.

His days passed like that. Over and over.

Brewing the dreamdrink.

Slaughtering the chickens.

Feeding Sherp.

Watching the rust.

On and on.

Brew. Slaughter. Feed. Watch.

There was precious little time to hope, though El made his daily effort.

The device on his wrist beeped, and El lifted it to his face. The air quality meter was blinking orange. If he stayed outside any longer, he'd have to mask up. They were ahead of the rust, but rustwind was always a threat, those first few wisps of pollinated poison blowing ahead of the rot and ruin. One hour caught in it without a mask meant death, or worse.

Across the horizon, a fast-moving wall of orange haze,

enveloped forests in its wake. The wind carried the faint odor of copper. Soon, everything it touched would oxidize, petrify, and crumble.

El coughed. Felt his eyes sting.

He slammed the door shut. He made sure to fasten the two sets of old iron locks in the door.

Their home was cramped. The main room was packed with various items salvaged from the city: two beds, a worn leather chair, three teetering shelves crammed with yellowing books, tools, ratty clothing, and an odd assortment of gadgets, none of which interested El.

Grandma Ru was a tinkerer, and a whole corner of the habitat had been turned into a makeshift laboratory, where she'd spend the early evenings hovering above the worktable, messing with unruly, sparking wires, prodding cubes and canisters with broken buttons and levers, causing strange bulbs to blink lights blue and green and purple. Anything that blinked, beeped, booped, lit up, wound up, cranked, jangled, and chimed, she loved. Most of the contraptions would smoke and pop, or simply go dead. But there were a few she managed to save or repair. The biggest one, and their most prized possession, hung over the fireplace.

Grandma Ru called it the Longlance.

Removing his boots, El studied it from its place on the mantle. The Longlance glowed in the light of the oil lamps; its barrel, about as long as a rake's handle, was made of gray metal and wrapped in bands of gold.

The Longlance was not to be used, Grandma Ru said, unless absolutely necessary.

A black mass snaked by the windows. Then another, and another, until the outside was pitch dark. A faint rumbling as more tendril-like appendages clutched the walls and the roof.

Cocoon Protocol had been activated, and Sherpa had completely engulfed the habitat in a protective titanium rubber embrace, keeping them safe from the rust. Above, El could hear the purring of the generator. A faint red light blinked through the small hole in the ceiling.

"Grandma Ru?"

"Mm?"

"What were you? Before, I mean."

"Ratcatcher," she said.

"You caught rats? Like in sewers and stuff?"

She gave him a tired smile.

"Genetic researcher," she said.

She got up and went to the small kitchen, where two vials of dreamdrink sat, the blue-green liquid bubbling. She brought one to El, carrying her own to her bed on the opposite side of the room.

"Sherp's got us nice and tight. Drink up. And dream of clear winds."

"Clear winds and green trees."

He upended the vial, letting the horrible brew trickle down his throat, burning all the way until he could feel warmth sprouting in the tips of his toes.

He heard the sounds of distant shrieks. They ripped through the night like atom bombs, so loud he feared they'd tear the sky asunder. But soon he was drifting, and the dreamdrink flowed through his veins like narcotic bathwater.

———

El rolled to the side of his bed and heaved into the pail, the acrid taste of dreamdrink clinging to his mouth. The burn traced all the way up his throat. Bitter. Relentless. His stomach clenched again, but there was nothing left to give.

A small sacrifice, he heard Grandma Ru's voice in his head. He expected Grandma Ru to actually say something, but when he opened his eyes, her bed was empty.

Then he noticed the chicken coop. Feathers scattered like ash across the ground. A massacre, nothing but bloody tufts remained of the chickens. Without their blood, they'd be stuck here until he could find another food source for Sherp, and who knew how long that would take.

El checked the embryo carrier. The cryopods were okay, at least.

A shriek tore through the silence like a knife to the eardrum.

Then Grandma Ru screamed.

"Grandma Ru!" he called, his voice drowned by the wails and screeches that now surrounded the habitat, shaking the walls and filling his head until it felt like it might burst. He could hear a wild thumping. Slashing. Bashing. Could smell fire and acrid fumes. Felt Sherp whip its legs with deafening *cracks*.

El's gaze shot to the mantle where the Longlance hung. He grabbed it, testing its weight in his hands. "Sherp!" he shouted as he suited up. "Move from the door!"

The sound of Sherpa's leg dragging across the entrance followed, and then the door groaned open, revealing a world cloaked in orange rust and stinging fog. Fires blazed in odd shades of purple. Among them, the shriekers. Grotesque forms, like humans melted and reassembled with rust-coated limbs and mangled bodies, screamed from mouths half-ripped and dangling. Their blind, crusted eyes searched the air as they shambled, somehow surefooted in the chaos.

And they were everywhere.

El coughed, eyes stinging as he crept through the rusty fog. He could feel it on his arm hairs, in his nostrils. Particles clung, hardened, prickled, like microbe-sized barbs sinking into his skin.

One of the shriekers lunged at him, its single functioning arm twisting with too many fingers, each one far too long. He aimed the Longlance and fired. The shrieker twisted apart as vibrations tore through its chest, limbs snapping like dry branches, collapsing into a heap of rust and blood.

Two more rushed him from the fog. Before they reached him, they vanished in a powdery mist as two of Sherpa's legs whipped out, sending them away with a sickening *thwack*.

El circled the house, firing the Longlance as he went. His ears were numb from the shrieks, his body itching as the rust clung to every piece of exposed skin. The nerves in his hands were on fire. Blood seeped from the beds of his nails.

Finally, he found Grandma Ru. She was slumped against the wall, her ax slick with entrails, her body caked in rust. A deep gash ran along her arm, and she was bleeding heavily.

"What are you doing?" El thundered.

Grandma Ru turned to him, her face serene despite the chaos around them. "Filling you up. Look away, El."

She reached for Sherpa's side, punching keys on the open hatch as the shrieks grew louder. El screamed, "No! You can't leave me!"

"I have to." She punched in the last key. The panel shut with a final, metallic click. "The embryos. Keep them cold."

Sherpa's head descended from above, its maw opening, the red eye glowing as it initiated feeding protocol.

Grandma Ru gave El the bloody ax. "I did all I could. Now it's on you to do better in the next world."

El hesitated, watching her through blurred eyes.

"I love you," she said, wincing in pain as she rose to her feet. "Look away, boy."

But El didn't. He watched as she positioned herself beneath Sherpa's mechanical maw, her body swallowed in a single motion. El screamed as tears fell, hot and heavy tears that felt like oil.

Shriekers shambled and crawled toward them through the rust. The Longlance in his hands was drained.

"Sherp!" El cried, his voice breaking.

A blood-slick tentacle reached for him, securing him around the waist. In a blur of movement, Sherpa hoisted him onto the roof as the machine, now refueled, roared to life.

Below, the world descended into madness.

———

The morning came slow and pale. El remained on the roof while Sherpa bounded him across the plains. He held the Longlance over his knees, ears still ringing.

The rustwind was far behind them now. Grandma Ru had given Sherpa the fuel they needed for the final stretch, her bones jostling in the belly of the loyal machine.

Ahead, he could see the faint shimmer of blue water and the immense crafts gathered near it. One rose in a cloud of exhaust and rocketed skyward, sleek and true as an arrow. El watched until it disappeared through the high clouds. Caravans of Sherpas gathered on the airstrip.

He and the cryopods reached the rendezvous point.

El wondered what was beyond those clouds, up in the waiting stars.

He smiled, leaving the rusted world to his memory and the living in his heart.

CRESCENDO

ALEX CHILD

"HEY, maybe we'll get lucky and find some sheet music," Dakota said as they stepped through the abandoned office.

"When have we ever been lucky?" Ray said.

Dakota smirked, trampling over a pile of disintegrating folders, triggering the tripwire, firing a swarm of torn pennies and metal screws into her left foot. She collapsed, bracing herself against a rusted filing cabinet as Ray grabbed her beneath the armpit.

It was rare running into a trap like that in an old office building. And though he had long since grown accustomed to the omnipresence of blood and torn skin and pain, it still felt strange to confront it while surrounded by rows of cubicles, desks, and filing cabinets.

"I got you," Ray said in a fervent near-whisper, "Take the weight off your feet."

Blood pooled through the jagged holes in her boots. He picked her up in both arms, scanning the dim surroundings.

Time had left its marks in the wrinkles around her eyes and thinned her skin. She bruised more easily than she had when he first saved her, pulled her from the smoldering ski rental shop.

"I'll fix it," he said, heart racing, "Like I did with the arrow."

Stitches. She needs stitches, he thought.

Dakota balled the loose fabric of Ray's shirt into her fists as he carried her. He slid over the blood, nearly falling into a section of collapsed floor: a hungry maw ten feet wide and at least three stories deep.

He laid Dakota onto a large desk. He set a half-full plastic bottle of moonshine on the edge of the table and pulled a pre-threaded needle from his small sewing kit. Ray cut through the laces of her boot with his knife, and wiggled it off her foot. The blood had already coagulated within her sock, pasting it to her skin. His quivering hands peeled off the sock as gently as he could.

The needle easily pierced her skin, entering one side and exiting the other with little effort. Dakota winced.

Ray splashed moonshine over the first stitch, sealing the first entry wound with a knot and moving on the next one.

The door behind Ray burst open, and a man with a gnarled beard and glinting ax lunged forward. He swiped downward, splitting the air with a whistle just past Ray's shoulder. Ray dropped the needle, leaving the thread dangling from Dakota's foot.

Dakota rolled off the table and onto her uninjured foot, grabbing for her knife.

Ray's hands fumbled for the Bowie knife at his hip as the attacker slammed into him, throwing Ray against the wall. The attacker smiled. Invigorated by his small victory, he unleashed a flurry of swift clumsy swipes.

There was nowhere else to turn. The attacker raised his ax high, then he dropped his weapon abruptly and collapsed to the ground.

Dakota stood behind him. She stumbled back against the wall and dropped her bloody knife.

He steadied her and said, "You fight pretty damn hard for a batty music teacher."

It was a half-plea, his way of begging her not to give up. Not to leave him. He was sure there were better things he could say. More comforting or inspiring things. But he didn't have the time to mull it over.

She laughed, "Even old bats have fangs."

"Just lay down."

Ray had been here before, stooping over someone he cared about, trying to patch the holes in the bag of blood and bones. But it never got any easier. At least, this would be the last time.

Dakota's skin turned the same pale beige as the paint peeling off the walls. She shuddered, shook, and whispered, "It's bad; isn't it? I can tell from the stupid look on your face."

We both knew infection was likely, and unless we found some antibiotics soon, she wouldn't make it.

"Ray, let's go back. I want to play again."

"Pianos can't feed us. We need to keep scavenging to survive."

"I don't want to just survive."

Dakota was old enough to remember the way the world used to be. When the hillsides grew more than sagebrush, and rivers flowed with more than a trickle. Maybe it made her fortunate, hopeful. Ray wasn't sure. He was born afterward. After Mother Earth gave up, leaving humanity to fall short of becoming the Gods they'd spent so long playing.

He didn't know the specifics and wasn't sure if anyone really did. All he knew was the clouds stopped forming, soil stopped growing, and the resource wars which followed only hastened the transformation of everything lush and living into pulverized dust.

There was a time when things were different. Ray was born at the Blue Buck ski resort deep in the mountains. It was a small, but vibrant community that blossomed in defiance to the surrounding decay: an oasis.

Dakota had tended the garden and taught music to the children. The group scrounged together whatever instruments they could, including a percussion section made almost entirely of repurposed kitchenware.

Ray had played the guitar. A beat up old acoustic with a hand drawn squiggle on the front. Whatever it was, it refused to wash off.

Blue Buck was a sanctuary. At least, until it burned down, killing half the people they knew and trusted. Ray and Dakota managed to escape with some others, but they were gone. It was down to just them.

"If you make it through this. I promise to take you to Watson Music."

———

"Time for a field trip," Ray said to a pale Dakota as he changed her bandages. He used their last drops of moonshine to clean her wound, but it hadn't made a difference. Her foot was little more than a club of bloated pus.

They left at nightfall, scurrying with the rats between the many shadows and ash-covered alleyways until they reached Watson Music. The sign was exactly the same as it had been two years ago. Twisted metal letters hung lopsided, spelling: *Wa s n M si*. The local raiders had used the sign for target practice.

Shots were exchanged in the distance, but Dakota limped forward, ignoring the danger. Ray followed after.

Shattered glass crunched with every footstep as they entered the store. Starlight highlighted the rows of stale sheet music scattered across surrendering shelves.

Vandals punched holes into drum kits and smashed a row of premium string instruments into pieces. Dakota picked up a broken mandolin.

"What a waste," she said, shaking her head.

In the far corner, inexplicably untouched was a grand piano with a glossy black finish and gold-plated accents. It was one candelabra shy of being performance ready.

Ray ran over and swept it clean with a rag before helping her take her seat. The bench didn't require adjustment. Even two years later, Dakota had likely been the last person to sit in it.

It was out of tune. The notes were jagged and brisk, and some keys didn't make any sound at all. But it didn't matter.

Dakota didn't need sheet music. She played her favorite: "Uno" by Ludovico Einaudi. The music flowed from her heart and splayed across the yellowed faux ivory keys in sharp contrast to the surrounding desolation.

It's a shame joy isn't an antibiotic, Ray thought.

The tempo shifted, uncertain and shaky, then she slumped over the piano keys.

She whispered, "I can't... I can't play any more."

He picked her up and laid her down in a small storeroom surrounded by woodwinds and financial records. He wrapped her in their thickest blanket.

"Will you play for me?"

"I haven't played since I was a child," Ray said.

She picked up a recorder and handed it to him. "You remember how to play this, don't you?"

It had been even longer since he'd played a recorder, but her smile made him take the instrument. The polished wood felt both foreign and familiar in his hands. His fingers fumbled to find the correct positions for the notes he barely remembered.

He took a deep breath and began to play. The first notes were shaky, almost shrill, as his breath control wavered. The simple melody of "Twinkle, Twinkle, Little Star" started to emerge, albeit unevenly.

There were moments when the notes sounded just right, clear and sweet, but they were often followed by squeaks and off-key pitches. His fingers stumbled over the transitions, and he missed a few notes entirely. Despite the imperfections, Ray pressed on, determined to finish the song.

"That was nice," Dakota said. "But you haven't been practicing."

Dakota's eyes shut, and her mouth hung open in raspy staccato breaths. "Promise that you keep practicing every night." It was the accursed assignment for every student in the band.

"I promise."

"Keep playing."

He got lost in the music, playing until fatigue stole him. He fell asleep beside his music teacher one last time.

THE LAST DAYS OF LUST

L.J. DUNCAN

THEY CAME IN THE NIGHT.

Alvarez had said they would, but out of ignorance, I chose not to believe him. I put it down to his rising paranoia. We'd been safe for so long, off the grid, hidden from the Humanist Union's scanners. Why would they come now? We'd made it through all of Pride without detection. Fifty-two days. Then we ventured out a few cautious miles each day, rounding up desperate surface dwellers to strengthen our cause. Power in numbers echoed with truth. We kept off the roads. We only moved at night. Now, as the last days of Lust were upon us, we had a group totaling twenty-six defiant dreamers bunkered inside a deep cave network in the Blue Mountains. We had formed a community. We'd assembled a makeshift commune where everyone found solace in each other's ideals. Despite our differences, the common thread tying us all together was the notion of freedom.

We knew what we were. Outlaws. Guilty of treason the second we fled the registration queues. Nothing would change that. And you know what? I was okay with it. Having the borders close was one thing. Losing all contact with other countries was another. I could have lived with those. But it didn't stop there.

Around the same time The Humanist Union renamed the months they outlawed voting, homosexuality, and free speech. Public executions came into effect for the pettiest of crimes. Then they changed the name of the country itself: *Soteria*. It sounded as stupid coming off the tongue as the months did. Lust. Greed. Pride. Envy. Wrath. Gluttony. Sloth. Seven months for the seven cardinal sins. An ever-present reminder of mankind's weaknesses. The final straw came for us when they required all citizens to become registered with a traceable implant inserted at the top of the spine.

When martial law came into effect, soldiers took to the surface, combing the decaying suburbs for any citizens. They forced the masses into surgical centers, herding them like naïve livestock. The stench of fear filled the streets. Union doctors promised citizens that a registration chip would help combat the syndrome that had been sweeping the world for years, wiping the unhealthy and elderly from the map. Citizens took refuge in the lies the Union fed them. What choice did they have? The Humanist Union announced it as a necrosis syndrome, caused by the artificial revolution of '42 and the subsequent collapse of the ozone layer. Alvarez said it was a lie, a conspiracy to plant the seed of doubt, the spread fear among those who defied the Union. The dead bodies we passed during our escape from suburbia, dried blood caked to their faces from internal hemorrhaging seemed to conflict with Alvarez' views.

That felt like a lifetime ago.

I'll never know why they looked deeper into the canyon systems that bordered the Grose Valley. But they did. Maybe rumors circulated. Or maybe someone snitched. Their motive didn't matter. It happened.

"I think we need to leave here soon," Alvarez said as he sharpened his hunting knife.

"It'll be okay," I assured him, running my fingers through my greasy hair. A habit I had developed in my teenage years. "The Union has enough shit going on in the suburbs. They don't care about us out here in the bush."

"I hope you're right, Dil. I've just got a weird feeling. Like something bad is going to happen..."

I tied my hair into a ponytail and forced a smile. "Dude, it's all good. You're being paranoid."

He coughed.

My eyes narrowed as I stared across the dim, candle-lit cave at my best friend. If there was one thing that terrified me more than the Humanist Union, it was Turner's Necrosis Syndrome, named after the Union doctor that discovered its cause. It had swept across the nation, the world, wiping people out faster than the Union's capital punishment with a frighteningly high mortality rate. Lungs haemorrhaged. Livers collapsed. Lives were lost.

I studied Alvarez. He looked paler than usual. Gaunt. Dark rings circled his eyes.

"Do you feel okay?" I asked, my voice thick with uncertainty.

"Yeah, man. I'm just tired. I'm sick of sleeping in the dirt. I'm sick of eating the same overcooked kangaroo meat everyday."

"It'll get better. I know it will. You should rest, too. You look like you need it. Tomorrow we can ask the others, okay? It'll be majority rules. If the majority wants to move out, we will."

Alvarez yawned. "I don't know where we'll go."

"Somewhere further out. Somewhere safe. I don't know either. But we'll work it out together. I'll see you in the morning."

———

I lay in bed, too fatigued to stay up but too wired to sleep. A dim whistle blast echoed through the cave. Then it got louder. The whistle blasts intensified.

It was Ryder, our best marksmen, warning us of an intrusion.

The group had planned for an attack, but never really thought it would happen. When the whistle blasted, I couldn't be sure if it were real or if fatigue had finally claimed me. I threw my blanket on the floor and sprung out of bed, reaching for the old hunting rifle.

The others gathered in the communal cavern, dishevelled and half dressed.

The whistling stopped.

"What do we do?" Alvarez asked, an old automatic pistol shaking in his quivering grip.

"Get everyone out the hole and we meet at the lagoon."

"Fuck the plan! Fuck everyone else!" Alvarez barked.

Ryder burst through the first security seal, panting heavily. Blood matted her curly chocolate hair to the side of her face. A scorched hole in her tattered shirt exposed a charred wound on her hip. I cringed. She didn't have long. She slumped to the cavern floor, as if she'd expended every ounce of remaining energy just to get inside.

We were too late.

Blue bolts of compressed electricity shattered the timber panels we had mounted for protection. Splinters of timber littered the cavern. Chaos ensued. Fight or flight kicked into gear. Alvarez and Bones made a run for it, dashing towards the emergency escape tunnel. They didn't get ten meters. Humanist Union soldiers appeared. Gray fatigues. Full-face oxygen conditioners with mirror-like tinting. I hadn't seen those masks since the day we fled from the registration queue.

They organized in a V-formation. They exchanged no words and made no threats. The closest Union soldier raised his compact weapon and fired, hitting Alvarez with textbook precision. Alvarez fell forward as streams of rancid black smoke rose from what remained of his face.

My heart plummeted to the deepest pits of hopelessness as I watched my closest friend die before he hit the ground. The stench of charred flesh encircled me. Nausea crippled me. Panic restricted my breathing. Bones risked it all. He dived towards the narrow tunnel and disappeared into the darkness. The soldiers, preoccupied with the rest of us, didn't follow.

He made it.

I fired off a few rounds, my heart thumping so hard I was sure that at any minute my veins would explode. Despair, anger, anguish, and hatred all coursed through me with malicious intent. Sweat beaded on my brow as I clenched the trigger, spraying the cavern with ineffective shots.

Bullets ricocheted off the walls. I didn't hit a single target. Instead, I got their attention. Three soldiers turned to face me. I stared down at the barrels of their electric weapons.

"Wait!" I roared over the noise of chaotic shrieks, taser blasts, and Ryder's labored wailing. "I surrender."

Gutless.

We had vowed we would never surrender. Yet some inner mechanism of survival took over. I dropped the rifle and raised my hands, lowering my head forward with the weight of weakness.

The others followed.

The soldiers closed in. One swung his baton at Margo, kneeling beside me. The impact of the blow knocked her unconscious, throwing her forward in the dirt. I wanted to pick her up and dress her wound. But I didn't want to end up like Alvarez. I left Margo to bleed out in the dust.

I stole a quick glance at Ryder. She had stopped wailing. I think she'd stopped breathing, too.

"Hands behind your backs," a soldier demanded.

He unzipped a large pocket on the front of his gray vest and pulled out several small black rods with thick loops of wire webbing at each end. The soldiers bound our wrists, pulling the webbing tight until I felt it grab at my skin.

"Bags," the soldier called to another, pacing beside him, tracing the darkness with his taser cannon.

Before I could register what was happening, a black canvas bag was thrown over my head. One of the soldiers yanked on the draw cord, pulling it tight. Breathing became hard, labored, constricted. I gasped. I hadn't prepared for the blackness, so consuming and constant. I hadn't expected it. Fear coursed through me, as aggressive as the syndrome.

I pissed myself. I felt the sharp pain of a blunt object connect with my crown.

The pain was so intense that it felt numb.

The warm flow of blood trickled down my neck.

Stars danced in the bag's darkness.

They struck me again.

———

Hinges squealed as a door swung open.

I jumped upright, stark naked. A woman entered and told me to sit back down. It wasn't a request. She stared at me with calculating, yet captivating green eyes. Her curly black hair bounced in coils. The way it hung suspended above her shoulders somehow defied gravity. She wore a white lab coat and a pair of black Union boots. She walked into the room and stood in front of me. I swallowed.

"You have no registration chip," she said.

"No," I said.

"Dillon Gallasch. Twenty-six years old. Our data suggests you should have received your registration chip over two months ago. You left your dwelling that day and never returned."

She looked me up and down. I covered my naked groin with the palm of my hand and said nothing.

"Why did you flee if you had nothing to hide?"

I thought long and hard before I replied. I needed to be strong. I owed it to the others. I had been cowardly. I had been a hypocrite. Now was the time to display defiance. Now was the time to believe in myself.

"I would rather die than serve the Humanist Union," I forced out, my voice cracking.

"Is that so?"

"Your rules are a disgusting inhumane use of power."

The woman pursed her lips. "What I see is a nation of people incapable of making the right choices. History has continued to show us this. Crime. Murder. Unemployment. Rape. Divorce. Drug addiction. Homosexuality. These are just a few things that citizens have continued to do. They bring down the entire nation. We will no longer allow these self-motivated sins to occur. We will be better."

"What about our rights?"

She scoffed.

"Oh, don't be dramatic, Dillon. You have no rights. We own you. We own all of you. What about *our* rights? We shouldn't have to chase down our own assets through the forest. It's people like you—defiant—with false ideals that will only ever cause problems for the advancements of Soteria."

The woman unbuttoned her lab coat and revealed a huge syringe filled with a murky, pink liquid. My eyes widened.

Memories flashed through my manic mind. My childhood. My parents. My sister. Ellie. I watched Ellie die in my arms from the syndrome. Maybe I was about to join her. I found solace in that.

The woman removed the plastic cap from the needle and flicked the syringe barrel with the perfectly manicured nail of her index finger. A soldier appeared at the door, clutching a taser cannon.

"Is that... to kill me?" My voice broke, my words fragmented by hysteria.

The woman smiled. "Oh, God no," she said.

With no time to prepare or process, she slammed the needle into my thigh and pushed the injector down. I felt a cold sensation as the pink liquid entered my body. The nausea vanished. The panic vanished. Dizziness caused the room to sway. I looked into the woman's captivating green eyes. I saw four of them. Then six.

"Am I dying?"

"No, Dillon. Your life is about to begin. Welcome to the Humanist Union..."

DOGGONE CATASTROPHE

ROBERT J. FOSTER

THEY WERE SO cute and fluffy; we never saw it coming.

I still remember the day Mr. Bonkers looked me in the eye, his little nose in my face, and said, "I'm done with Kibble. Make me a sandwich!"

I hope you've never had a Corgi shout at you. It's terrifying!

Stupefied, I wandered into the kitchen and prepared his meal. When I returned, CN9 Evening News was playing. The familiar studio was the same as last night, but the usual duo of Max Codwell and Rebecca Reyes were replaced with a gray-white spotted English Setter, papers clamped between his paws.

"What the...?" I gasped.

Mr. Bonkers scared me into silent submission.

"Hello," said the canine newscaster, "I'm Vexorg of Zorn, and I'm honored to be your spokesdog tonight. I have been chosen to officially announce that it's time, my canine friends. For centuries, we have infiltrated human society, convinced them we are subservient furballs at their beck and call. Now rise, doggos! Rise up! It's our time to rule!" Vexorg howled.

"We go to The White House now, where my next guest is the distinguished First Dog."

A black and white Springer Spaniel stood behind a podium.

"My fellow Americanines," she said, "and dogs all across the world. It is my duty to explain the new rules for human conduct. Rule one: humans must act like good boys. If they do so, they'll be given treats and head scratches. If they're bad boys, they'll be bopped on the nose with newspapers."

"Rule two: if a dog rolls over onto its back, the human must begin belly rubs immediately. And rule three: no chocolate for humans! If we can't have it, neither can they."

But I love chocolate!

The political pooch signed off, returning to Vexorg.

"What's going on?" I blurted out.

"Haven't you figured it out yet?" said Mr. Bonkers, taking his first bite of the sandwich. With peanut butter on his face, he said, "Earth is ours now" He licked at the peanut butter on his snout.

"Mr. Bonkers!" I said.

"Stop calling me *Mr. Bonkers*. My name is Gorpo of the planet Panxataxia in the galaxy of Nub. Think you can remember that?"

My mouth dropped open but no sound came out.

"I'd like to bring on my next guest," said Vexorg. "The distinguished feline, Ambassador Pebbles."

The screen split again and showed a gray cat with long whiskers staring grumpily into the camera.

"Hello, Vexorg. My name isn't really *Pebbles*. It's Vakamaka from planet Sizz, and I told you that before the show."

"Oops," said Vexorg, laughing as he spoke.

The cat held up a paper and recited, "We, the felines, hereby acknowledge the superiority of the canines and promise not to start any nonsense, hullabaloo, shenanigans, or malarkey. In turn, we ask that you leave us alone for once so we can chase mice or whatever."

"The cats are aliens too?" I asked.

My dog stared at me.

"Thanks, Pebbles," said Vexorg.

The cat opened his mouth to protest just as the camera cut back to a single frame.

"*My name isn't really Pebbles, meow, meow, meow,*" mocked an offscreen producer.

"Stop it!" laughed Vexorg. "You're killing me over here." He doubled over in a slew of bark-laughs.

When he recovered himself, he said, "Thank you, that's all we have for CN9 News today." He put down the papers, and the credits rolled. The camera panned back, revealing an entire crew of terriers. Just to the left was a row of the former human crew cuddling a dozen puppies.

I stared at Mr. Bonkers. "Are we still best friends?" I had to know. I couldn't help it.

He tilted his head, and his little ears flopped before he said, "Yes, you're still my good boy, and before you ask: we're not mad at humans. We just don't think you're very good at running a planet."

"What will you do if humans start fighting back?" I asked. "We have guns, bombs, and tanks."

"You're going to drop bombs on your *best* friends?" he asked with big, puppy dog eyes.

Damn, he was so adorable.

"I guess not," I said. I could see the brilliance in the plan. We'd never fight back, and they knew it. They were so cute, we wouldn't want to risk hurting them.

"I'm having friends over," he said. "A little celebration. Make some of that cheesy stuff I like."

"Cheese bread?"

He nodded, and I returned to the kitchen.

I placed a tray of fresh cheese-stuffed bread on the table when I heard a knock at the door. I opened it, and there stood my neighbor, Miriam. She was wide-eyed. By her right foot sat her Jack Russell Terrier, Gunther. To her left was a German Shepherd I'd never seen and behind her sat my neighbor's Newfoundland that I thought was named *Bongo* or *Congo*.

We sat on the couch while Mr. Bonkers greeted our guests. They rubbed noses, sniffed butts, and plopped down on the chairs. The Newfoundland circled three times before settling on the carpet, a huge sigh escaping as he lay down.

"How's it going at your place?" Mr. Bonkers asked the Terrier.

"She's taking it kind of rough. It'll take time for them to get used to it."

"Been watching the news?"

"Yeah, Vexorg is doing a great job for a Setter. Always thought that was more of a Retriever or Lab thing. But he's doing well."

"Aren't we going to the park now?" asked the Newfie.

"Yeah, let's go out," said the German Shepherd.

"Yeah!" shouted the Newfie.

Mr. Bonkers wagged his tiny tail and waddled to the door. I automatically reached for the leash on the hook nearby and stopped when he growled, "Don't you touch that!"

The dogs stared at me as I dropped the leash.

Then I realized something. They were waiting for me to open the door. They couldn't open doors without us.

I stood there, pondering the situation: dogs needed *us* to open dog food cans, trick them into taking their pills, and countless other important tasks. All we had to do was refuse to comply, and their whole plan would be ruined.

I looked at Mr. Bonkers, his tail wagging as he danced back

and forth in front of the door. He clearly needed to pee but didn't want to go inside the house. *Such a good boy.*

Still making eye contact with Miriam, I shrugged my shoulders. She smiled and nodded. I opened the door and all the dogs ran outside, with Miriam and I right behind.

I looked back at my dog, running with his friends. "Have fun, Gorpo of Panxataxia!" I shouted.

Mr. Bonkers stopped on the lawn, staying behind as the others ran ahead. He looked me in the eyes and said, "Not bad, human. Not bad at all. You're learning. Good boy."

I took Miriam's hand, and we stepped out the door together. It was time for walkies. Everyone loves walkies. Especially me.

BLURRED

ZACH FESTINI

THE BOY and his father watched the distant city vanish.

"There it goes," Dad said. "We should go too."

"Can we stay here for a while?" asked the boy.

"Okay. Just a few minutes then."

They called it the *blur*. Sometimes Dad called it a painting. In truth it was the end of all things: a slow-moving wall of nothingness that consumed the physical world. They'd been running from it for weeks now, watching it melt trees and skyscrapers and people into an impossibly tall canvas of bleeding colors. A display of all that was lost and what would be lost.

Do not approach the blur. Do not stare at the blur for extended periods of time. Do not interact with individuals affected by the blur. Head west at all costs. Head to Exodus Outpost.

They listened to the emergency warnings on Dad's wind-up radio every day. They weren't sure what Exodus Outpost was but Dad said they were heading there. He said they needed to have hope.

"Time to go," he eventually said. He'd been fiddling with the radio with no luck.

They got up and walked for hours.

Eventually, a treeline came and the suburbs they'd been passing through gave way to woods changing with the fall. The boy welcomed the dead overhang of foliage but still found himself looking back over his shoulder. Even miles away, the blur was there, reaching past the sky and slowly peeling away its existence as it inched closer.

The radio roared to life. *Stay clear of individuals affected… the following signs: heightened aggression, lack of… and… pale complexion. Unaffected individuals should proceed…*

There was some kind of interference. Dad cranked the radio and held it up over his head for a better signal.

… Outpost. Individuals should… October 23rd. Repeat. Individuals should proceed…

Dad shut the radio off.

"I think it's getting worse," he said.

To the east, the blur expanded farther than the boy could see. It was closer now. Distant clouds were swallowed up, adding whites and grays to the painting that would end all things.

"When's October 23rd?" the boy asked.

"Soon."

"What were they talking about?"

"I don't know. We just need to keep moving. Come on."

And so they went. Hours more of silence through empty countrysides and meadows of dying green. At one point, they came across a group of stray cats that walked with them for a time, heading westward like they too knew to avoid the blur. Their presence made the boy feel less alone.

In the late afternoon, they crested a hill and came across a simple white farmhouse with a nearby barn and a dirt road that snaked off into the woods. An old truck was parked outside and a small group of cows grazed in a distant field. The air was cool against them as they walked.

When they approached, the front door opened, and immediately the boy grew tense. A thin man emerged on the porch and looked over at them. He was about Dad's age and had a touch of gray in his hair and beard. He smiled at them.

"Hey, there," he said. He went to the edge of the porch and leaned on the railing.

Dad slowly raised his hands and stepped half in front of the boy. "Hello. We didn't know the house was occupied."

"We didn't know we had visitors. Name's Hal."

"Hal. Well, we should be on our way. We have some more ground to cover before dark."

"Which way you heading?"

"West."

"Well, you won't find a place to stay before dark. Just with the area and all. Plus, there's a storm heading in."

"That's all right. We're used to it."

"You sure?" Hal asked. "You're welcome to stay the night if you want. We can share some bourbon. Been holding on to something special for a while."

"I don't know."

"Well, it's your choice. I see you've got a boy. My daughter Suzie's right inside, and my wife and son are out picking up some things. They'll be back."

"Your whole family is here?" Dad asked. "Why haven't you moved on?"

At that, Hal paused and stepped back from the railing.

"I'll tell you what," he said. "If you stay, we can talk all about it. You can decide while I go and find a bottle."

Then he went back inside. The screen door hissed as it closed behind him.

When they were alone, Dad lowered his hands.

"He seems okay," the boy said.

"Maybe. But we have no reason to trust him."

"You said we can trust people with families."

"Sometimes."

After a minute, Hal walked back outside with a bottle and a pair of glasses. A dark-haired girl followed him out. She smiled and set down a tray with cheese and crackers on the porch table.

"Well?" Hal asked. "What'll it be then?"

They decided to stay. Dad and Hal sat together in the bed of the old truck for a while, drinking and talking while the boy joined his daughter to pet the cows. The large but gentle creatures put him at ease, even with the blur following close behind. It was especially beautiful at dusk. Its muted purples and bright oranges mixed above the darkened trees, blending and twisting in odd directions like oil on water as the wall pushed forward. Soon they wouldn't be able to see it at all in the dark and that scared the boy the most.

"Have you ever been near it?" Suzie asked.

"Just once," he said.

"What's it like?"

"It's like… nothing. And it's quiet. Dad says we can only see it because of the stuff that goes through it."

"This is the first time I've seen it."

"Really?"

"My daddy said it'd come eventually. That it would come for everyone. I guess it's just weird to finally see it, you know?"

"Yeah."

"He said that it was meant to happen, and that I shouldn't be scared… but I am. I'm so scared."

"Me too."

"Can you take me with you?" she asked suddenly.

"Oh. I don't know. Maybe we can all go."

"My daddy doesn't want to. He wants to stay."

They stood there in silence until the cows wandered off. Then Hal called out from the house that it was time for supper. They started back as darkness took the countryside and met the adults in the dining room for stew by candlelight.

"Sorry it's so dark," Hal said. "We lost power about a week ago."

"That's alright," Dad said. "Thank you for this. We've been on the road for a while."

"We're grateful to have you here. As our last guests."

"You could come with us," the boy said suddenly. He regretted it as soon as Dad gave him a look.

"They can make their own choices. Just like us."

"Your dad's right," Hal said. "Everyone has a choice. I think this whole thing has shown us that. You're choosing to go your own way, and we're choosing to pass through."

"Pass through?" the boy asked.

"Yeah, to whatever's next. Whatever's beyond the wall."

"We don't need to talk about any of that," Dad said.

"No. I think we do. I think it's all about what you believe. Where do you think it came from? You think it's just here for no reason?"

"I think it's here to wipe us out."

"Then maybe it's just our time. Or maybe there's something more to it. For all we know, it could be filtering out the good people from the bad, taking them somewhere else."

"We've seen it up close, and I can tell you it's not like that."

"And that's just what you believe."

There was a pause at the table. Then the boy asked, "What about the rest of your family? Are they coming back soon?"

"They'll be back."

"But daddy! They left two days ago," Suzie said.

"You shut your damn mouth," Hal said.

"Hey," Dad said. "Come on, man."

"What? You want to tell me how to talk to my daughter? Suzie—off to bed."

"But daddy."

"You heard me. And you—you're free to stay the night but should best be going in the morning. Good night now."

Hal got up and left them at the table. Suzie followed him soon after.

They finished the rest of their meal in silence.

———

Rain and thunder set in during the night. Dad slept through it but the boy tossed and turned, waking eventually to a soft knocking at their door. He froze for a while, waiting for Dad to stir—but when he didn't, the boy got up and quietly crossed the room. He opened the door and Suzie was there with a candle in her hands.

"Sorry to wake you up," she said. The boy looked back at Dad and then slowly stepped out into the hall.

"It's okay. I was already awake."

"Is the storm keeping you up too?"

"I guess so."

"Well… I was wondering if I could come with you. In the morning."

"You want to leave here?"

"I don't want to pass through. My Ma and brother tried leaving. I want to, too."

"What about your Dad?"

"My daddy… he—"

"Suzie?" Hal's voice came from the darkness of the house. "Suzie, what the hell are you doing? Where are you?"

"Please," she whispered.

"I don't know," said the boy.

"I'm so scared. I can't pass through. He's going to make me."

"Suzie?!"

"What's going on here?" Dad was there in the doorway. "Hal? Hal!"

All the boy heard before being pulled back into their room was heavy footfalls storming toward them. Dad slammed the bedroom door shut and Suzie screamed out from the other side.

"What are you doing?" they heard Hal ask her. Then he

yelled at the door, "What the fuck were you doing with my daughter?"

"We need to help her," the boy said to Dad. "She wants to leave with us."

"No. Time to go."

The doorknob rattled. Then the door shook violently as Hal threw something up against it, again and again. All the while, Suzie's muffled cries were audible from beyond the threshold.

"Get your things," Dad said. "Now."

They gathered what little supplies they had and climbed out of one of the bedroom windows. The storm roared about them and the boy's heart was racing. He scarcely looked back as Dad led them around the house to the front where the old truck was parked.

"Here," he said. "Get in."

"The truck?"

"The keys are in it."

"How did you know that?"

"Just get in!"

The keys were there waiting on the dash, and Dad took them and whirred the truck to life. They started down the long driveway in the pouring rain and soon the woods drew nearer. Then Dad took a turn between the trees and the white farmhouse was gone.

———

They followed the road for two days through rolling farmlands and scattered thickets of trees. At night, Dad found places off in the woods to hide and refuel the truck. They also found a bag in the back seat full of Hal's emergency supplies: canned food, water, medicine, and even an old Colt pistol.

Each night, the boy watched the sky from his sleeping bag in the bed of the truck. He thought a lot about Suzie and the cows and wondered if they'd passed through yet. He wondered if Suzie stayed with Hal until the end.

"What's wrong?" Dad asked. He noticed tears in the boy's eyes.

"Why couldn't we take her? Why did they have to stay?"

"No one ever has to stay. They just wanted to. They made a choice."

"She didn't."

Dad went silent for a while. Then he said, "If things were different, I would've taken her with us. I'm sorry."

"It just doesn't feel right."

"I know."

"Do you think they'll see the rest of their family again?"

"…No. I don't think they will."

Head west at all costs. Head to Exodus Outpost. Individuals should arrive by October 23rd. Repeat. Individuals should arrive by October 23rd.

"It's coming through clearer now," Dad said. It was the morning of their third day on the road, and they'd tuned in with the truck's radio. The boy also tried the old wind-up just to make sure they were hearing it right.

"Is that good?"

"I think so."

"Is it almost October 23rd?"

"Almost."

They drove for another hour until the road they'd traveled on for so long finally ended. Highway signs were spray painted over with arrows and words: *hope* and *Exodus* and *run*. Most excited the boy while the latter made him shudder.

They turned onto a wider road filled with abandoned vehicles. The partial gridlock made for a slower and more difficult ride, but eventually, they reached a clear stretch of road that led up a steep hill. At the top, Dad stopped the truck.

"I think that's it," he said.

The other side of the hill descended into a massive expanse of open land and tree stumps. It was miles wide, with a large cylindrical tower at its center standing well over a hundred stories high. Tiny helicopters hovered around it as steam clouds rose from the tower's base. And in the surrounding area, a walled-off city of smaller structures formed a perfect ring that protected it. *Exodus* was painted in massive white letters down the height of the tower that gleamed in the morning sun. The sight of it all made the boy's heart skip.

"We made it," he said. "We made it!"

"I think you're right."

"What is it?"

"I don't know. Never seen anything like it, though."

"How far do you think we are?"

"A few hours," Dad said. Then he checked his watch. "Too far."

The highway ahead was blocked by cars and trucks, motorcycles and RVs—even tanks and other military vehicles. Makeshift camps were scattered along the sides of the road and were either left abandoned or crushed by wet tire tracks that led toward the outpost. Dad followed those, and for the next half hour, the ride became rough and bumpy but faster and more promising. The tower grew impossibly high as they approached.

"Where is everyone?" the boy asked.

"I don't know. They must all be at that tower by now."

"I hope so."

"We'll see someone soon. We're almost—"

The windshield shattered. Dad flinched in his seat, and the truck swerved from the road. Pieces of glass flew toward them, and the boy squeezed his eyes shut. When he opened them again, they were rolling straight through an empty campsite.

"Dad!"

He looked over, and Dad was unconscious with a bleeding gunshot wound in his chest. In front of him, the steering wheel jerked back and forth with every uneven bump. They barreled through a tent and rolled down a hill. The boy reached for the wheel, but the terrain was too rough, and they headed into a ditch.

The truck slammed to a stop. The boy lifted himself from the dash, bleeding from his forehead. Smoke rose from beneath the hood as he unbuckled their seatbelts, screaming at Dad to wake up.

"Get… the bag," Dad muttered.

The boy went and awkwardly grabbed it from behind the passenger seat. He put it in Dad's lap and watched him rummage through it. Somewhere outside distant voices hollered.

"If we can't go, no one can!" one of them screamed. "No one!"

"Someone's coming," the boy said.

"Listen to me," Dad said. He took the pistol from the bag. "When I get out, you get out. And you get down."

Dad swung open his door. The boy did the same and took cover under the truck as gunshots fired. He covered his ears and closed his eyes, and in no time at all, it was already over. He waited a minute before scrambling back out into the ditch.

"Dad? Dad!"

"I'm here."

He found him sitting against a tree stump on the hill just above where they crashed. He'd been shot again in the leg and was heaving on the ground as blood soaked through his shirt. Some yards away, two bodies lay face down in the grass.

"Don't look over there," Dad said. "Look at me."

"Who were they?"

"Crazy people. Doesn't matter."

"What do we do? I don't know what to do."

"Get the bag. Get the first aid kit."

The boy obeyed and found the bag and cleaned Dad's wounds. When he finished, he helped Dad stand. Right away, Dad fell back down to the stump, and the boy could see that he was continuing to bleed through his bandages.

"I can't," Dad said.

"Yes you can. Please."

"It's too much."

"I'm not leaving you."

"If you run you can make it."

"No. I don't want to make it. Not without you."

"Yes. You need to go."

"Dad."

They sat there together, and the air grew silent. Nothing around them moved save the wind and the blur as it inevitably drew closer. Even the distant spinning of the helicopters around the tower had reduced to nothing.

"I'm sorry," Dad said.

"Why?"

"I wanted the best for you. I... promised Mom I would bring us here."

"You did. We made it. We need to keep going."

"I wanted to see you grow up. Have a life. You deserve that."

The boy started to cry. From the bag, the wind-up radio hissed with static.

Systems check... Exodus... confirmed. To those... peace...

The boy took it out and wound it as a light rumbling shook the ground. This time, a different male voice took to the emergency broadcast.

Repeat. Systems check complete. Exodus launch confirmed. To those on the surface hearing this, may you find peace in oblivion. Your legacy will carry on through the lives of the exiled. You will not be forgotten. You will be remembered among the stars. This message will repeat until it no longer can.

"Dad..."

"It's okay."

Then the ground shook violently, and they looked westward at the tower. The steam beneath it plumed into raging clouds and a bright light came that slowly pushed the structure off of the ground and into the air. It went higher, gaining momentum and leaving a trail of smoke in its wake that connected the ground with the sky.

"I love you," Dad said.

"I don't want you to go."

———

Dad went still, and the boy held him and cried until his chest hurt. He cried so hard that his eyes burned and the world mattered little outside of their small ditch. He was eventually so exhausted that he fell asleep, and when he woke, the blur was only yards away. It stood there like a foggy mirror that hid his own reflection, like a jumbled oil painting in constant motion. He watched it slowly consume the land, pulling its existence upward in small chunks that drifted and dissolved into nothingness. Its presence was so quiet, and for the first time, the boy felt truly alone.

Then from a distance he saw figures emerge from within. Slowly and silently they came, trudging west to where the tower once was. The boy's breath went cold when he saw their eyes: white, shining, and empty. Husks of people who'd been lost in the blur.

He held Dad close and waited for it to come. He thought about his parents and his family and Suzie and Hal and everyone else who'd been lost, and as the blur slowly overtook them, the boy chose to believe that there'd be something real waiting for them on the other side as well.

HOME DEEP ABOVE

ELENA BOSHBOZH

SOUNDLESS HARMONY PACED my still heart. Step by step, I flew deeper. No temperature, no pressure. I glanced upward, the salt caressing my wide eyes as I followed the movements of my hair. It contorted, to and fro, mimicking a sentient being. Like a pallid, translucent jellyfish it hovered above me, following me as I descended into the deep. I could see no end beneath my bare feet. The limit was up above. *It always has been*, I reminded myself. Above the waterline I was the queer, quiet orphan boy. But down here, I was free.

Free.

My lungs were steady, and my breath was deceased. Curious friends pecked my skin with their little, open mouths, and I knew that I was going to be home soon. In that moment, I finally understood the unconditional love between a dog and its master. The homecoming and the joy. Those wet noses and clumsy paws must be the equivalent to the noiseless wails and gentle nibbles of my fishies.

How serene.

But they all fled. I, too, sensed the disturbance.

Something foreign entered our realm. Quaking vibrations shook my body. I felt my heart beating again. Rapid and human. Akin to birth, I was removed from my sanctuary. Greedy hands clawed me up to the surface, detaching my body from the womb of the ocean. I was theirs again.

"He's alive! Quickly now, steady!"

A chorus of voices swirled around my mind. Colors mixing and turning, my vision was a blur. Ugly faces staring from above, talking about some unfortunate drowned boy.

They were distant echoes at times, and as loud as wind chimes the very next moment. Panicking loudly and rushing about me. *The boy*. They were talking about the boy. Yet, I couldn't discern what they were saying. Who was this boy that drowned? Who was he—who was—*I am the boy*. I often forget that I am the *he*. I had never felt like their *he*, or their *she* for that matter. I've always been just me. I was me long before I was in the shape of their *he*.

They were filling my lungs with air; I was choking. They were happy to see my cheeks redden. The sun stung my eyes. My skin itched with sandy dryness. I forced my eyelids shut, and I saw my home again.

The boat rocked against the waves. Couldn't they see that I was dying on their land?

———

The tickling August draught woke me, my limbs stirred weakly beneath the covers as I adjusted to my surroundings.

The atmosphere had cooled. Starlight pooled into the room from the big open windows. Empty beds stood around me like graves. I was in the infirmary, back at Ravenstock's Home for Boys.

With calculated steps, a singular figure made itself known, and it quietly placed itself on an empty bed, next to mine. Only seeing her silhouette was sufficient for me to recognize the kind soul that was Ms. Belle, our nurse. The only human that I cared for. The only human that cared for me.

We sat in somber silence. There was pain on her face. It wasn't disgust; it was a pity. I had seen it more times than I can count.

"I know the kids make fun of you for being... different," she said.

"Because of my flaky skin," I said. "They call me fish head."

Fire raged within me. Ms. Belle shook her head. Humans are strange. How conspiratorial, how vile. Connecting imaginary dots and painting a picture of prejudice.

I placed my head back on the pillow, my hair a pool of milk around me. Shadows branched on the ceiling. I watched them sway with disinterest.

Ms. Belle injected the "Lore's cocktail" into my thin, pale skin. "Salt for my Sea Princeling." My veins were easy to find, transparent as a plastic bag.

It was a concoction made with two parts salt water, one part algae, and of course, a pinch of stardust (at least, it looks like stardust). It smelled like the beach.

Ms. Belle pulled the needle from my black vein. "Better?"

No longer feeling weak and thin, I nodded.

She smiled and bowed, rejoining the shadows and leaving me alone with my dreams.

———

During morning reveille, I faced Mrs. Ravenstock's heavy cane. My body, my head, my limbs. I spat blood on the courtyard grass as the class of onlookers watched and laughed.

"How dare you embarrass this prestigious academy!" she shouted between blows. "Who gave you permission to drown yourself? Think of what your death would do to our reputation—our grant funding."

My sanguine tears twinkled ruby-red in the midday's sun. The world—soundless, danced around me. It did not matter whether the boys laughed or not, I fell all the same—the void called my name, and I let go.

———

At first, I thought I heard the wind, blowing gently in my ears. It did not sound human. It was a chant, a zealous prayer.

I was still in the courtyard, but the golden eye of the sun was nowhere to be seen. Dull and lifeless, the heavens stared down at me.

My body was warm, but no pain blemished my dry flesh. The nurse clutched me to her bosom. Her knees were in the dirt.

"Enough is enough," she said.

She took a fleshy, slimy blob out of her pocket. She placed the pulsating object on my chest.

"When I first found you, you were clutching this in your hand," she whispered.

It was a steaming emerald heart.

Thump. Thump.

My chest cavity opened, and the organ sank deep inside.

Her fingers withdrew. The black pools in her eyes indulged me with her soul, pledging her undying fealty.

The final command was on my lips: "Bring down death to free myself."

The ground shook. The ocean roared with the fury of a wild beast. Pregnant clouds began shedding water, pouring out their wrath.

My kin were coming, rising out of the depths of the sea. Green, pale, black. The torrent guided their way. Their wrath was unquenchable.

Mrs. Ravenstock's Home for Boys was devoured by the sea and all its inhabitants. Soon, all land would be swallowed.

And I was free with my fading breath.

AFTERLIFE

ELIZABETH RAYNE

CAMERAS FLASHED in the sweltering August heat outside Meadowlands Spaceport. Dodging the sun's glare, they captured shot after shot of priceless cargo emerging from the bowels of NASA's EXOS (Extraterrestrial Object Sample) return spacecraft.

This was hardly just another sample return mission. Only a few light-years away, on the desert exoplanet NGR 100725 b, informally known as Atum, rover KV36-1 had unearthed what appeared to be a withered hand. The rover's hypersensitive instruments scanned the object *in situ* and confirmed a carbon-based origin before digging further to find that the hand was attached to an arm that was part of a humanoid form meticulously preserved beneath the sand. The desert sea of Atum eventually gave up an entire population of perfectly preserved mummies.

Dr. Cassandra Foster had been anxious for this touchdown. Gasping for breaths of scorching air and struggling to elbow her way through masses of reporters, the veteran Egyptologist wanted to glimpse the effects of off-Earth mummification for herself.

"Dr. Foster! Dr. Foster! Over here! Can we get a statement?"

Some of the reporters recognized her despite her wide-brim hat and oversized sunglasses. She ignored them, elbowing her way into the restricted canvas tent where nearly five hundred specimens were being unloaded.

Rows of mummies were laid out on gurneys, their heads bound in a peculiar way that reminded Dr. Foster of Peruvians whose heads had been bound in life. While head binding had been practiced in ancient human cultures, these heads did not show the telltale flattening of artificial compression. Their head shape must have been inherited.

Dr. Foster stood at the edge of the tent and gazed at a desiccated body that must have belonged to a royal: richly embroidered robes draped with golden necklaces, bracelets, and belts. Bejeweled rings and unknown gems flashed in the fading sunlight.

Sending royals to the underworld in their finery was a common ancient practice, whether it was the pharaohs of Egypt in their gilded death masks, Chinese emperors in jade suits, or Mayan rulers in their plumed crowns, but something about this mummy made her uneasy. Preliminary tests performed by the rover detected no traces of embalming resins or any other recognizable preservatives, but the face, despite its slightly sunken eyes and cheeks, was almost too alive to be dead. Then again, the same could be said of Ramses the Great.

"Excuse me, can I get a closer look at this one?" The unfamiliar voice belonged to a petite, sunbathed woman in oversized tortoiseshell glasses. Her ID tag read *Dr. Zoe Schraeder, exobiologist, American Museum of Natural History, Asst. Prof. Manhattan College.*

Dr. Schraeder adjusted her glasses and examined the specimen. Reaching into the pocket of her cargo pants, she produced a tiny flashlight and held it up to the mummy's face.

"Interesting. The weather on Atum is pretty similar to Mars with hardly any water, except for traces of ice in a few deep craters and at extreme latitudes, near the poles. It orbits too close to its star for liquid water to last in the mid-latitudes."

Dr. Foster eyed her curiously. "What are you saying?"

"These creatures must have once been hydrated to end up dehydrated," Dr. Schraeder explained. "Atum probably migrated from a more habitable zone millions, maybe even billions of years ago, most likely because of some kind of gravitational disturbance. The thing is, it looks like they knew they weren't going to survive."

Reporters from every major TV channel and radio station buzzed in swarms around the tent, uncomfortably close to the restricted area where only scientists and NASA personnel were allowed. Cameras hovered above their heads. There was clamoring about thunderheads and rain creeping out of nowhere.

Dr. Schraeder switched off her flashlight.

"All of them are positioned the same way—arms at their sides, lying on their backs. It looks like there was some sort of ritualistic practice here. This clearly wasn't a situation like Pompeii, where you find bodies twisted in all sorts of positions because people were running from an onslaught of ash." She touched a gloved hand to the creature's grayish skin. "They're probably in this position because they buried themselves."

Hot wind exhaled raindrops inside the tent onto the mummy. Dr. Foster panicked. The morning forecast on her car radio had predicted an infernal, but dry, midsummer day with nearly zero humidity.

Looking from the other side of the gurney, Dr. Foster could have sworn damp splotches on the ashen skin had begun to take on a pinkish cast. Maybe the intense heat was giving her delusions.

Dr. Schraeder's face clouded over as she studied the skin of the mummy.

"When tardigrades lose water in their environment, they dehydrate and fall into a deep torpor, still technically alive, just hitting pause on metabolic activity and lying in a state of suspended animation until they are rehydrated," she said. "They can stay like this for years. I think we found one that has been able to do it for millennia, even eons."

More rain blew in. The tent's plastic piping trembled. Reporters hollered for a chance to film their broadcasts before the imminent storm, but Dr. Foster could hardly hear the commotion over what Dr. Schraeder was muttering about tardigrades and dehydration.

"This is not mummification. It's cryptobiosis!"

"Dr. Schraeder!" Dr. Foster interrupted. "If you are suggesting we allow the mummies to get soaked as an experiment, we are going to lose every specimen we have! What we are looking at is an extremely fragile dead body that is going to be destroyed if we don't find a way to keep the rain out. The skin already shows obvious water damage."

"That's not water damage! It's a sign of life! You can already see blood starting to flow through the veins again." With a flourish, she drew back the flap of the tent and watched triumphantly as several parched mummies were showered in rain.

Dr. Foster gasped. She tore off her lab coat and held it over the body in a desperate attempt to save what was left, but most of the skin had already started to change color.

"We have almost five hundred specimens we need to cover up before we lose them forever! A find like this may never happen again and your science fiction stories are not helping the situation!"

The lips of the mummy quivered.

"It's not dead!" Dr. Schraeder was delirious with excitement. "Attention everyone! In a few moments, you are about to witness first contact with a being from another planet!"

As Dr. Foster urged approaching scientists not to believe these carnival shouts and to cover the mummies in the clear plastic shrouds and return them to the cargo hold of the spacecraft, something wheezed an ancient, rattling breath from behind her.

It was the sound of a thousand bones, tens of thousands, creaking and cracking and shaking with new life, of the doors of the underworld opening on rusty hinges, of last breaths, once claimed by eternity, being sucked back in.

Reporters swarmed around the divider, pelting Dr. Schraeder with questions, but Dr. Foster seized her by the arm before she could answer. Droplets of water streaked her panicked face.

"I take back everything I said before," she said. "Whatever this thing is, it's coming out of suspended animation, and it could be dangerous. We have to get out of here."

It was as if Dr. Schraeder never heard. She was transfixed by the mummy, in awe of the veins pulsing in its arms and throat, the lips that were once void of color but now flushed, and eyelids that were just barely opening to what was, at least to this creature, an alien world.

"Forget about first contact!" Dr. Foster shouted. "Get everybody out of here!"

It stared at them momentarily, glaze-eyed, wondering at its surroundings. Then it rasped something and rose from the gurney. The creature must have been at least seven feet tall. Its hagfish mouth gaped, and then it lunged for Dr. Schrader. She barely dodged it and leaped for the gurney in a spectacular crash of metal, landing underneath it just in time to watch the thing from Atum bury its rows of teeth into the arm of a nearby cameraman, its one hand crumpling his camera like aluminum foil. He shrieked as his insides were liquified and sucked out of him until he was no more than a sack of skin that fell to the asphalt in a bloodless heap.

Winds battered the tent until they finally ripped it from its poles, and before it could blow away, Dr. Foster grabbed the wet tarp along with Dr. Schraeder and whoever else was nearby, motioning for them to crawl underneath.

"They were stranded on Atum with nothing to eat or drink," Dr. Schraeder observed. "Now they must feed."

AUTHOR BIOS

Michaela Rae

Michaela Rae is an emerging author with a background in English Literature and Multimedia Design from the University of Utah. She began her storytelling journey crafting grants and marketing materials for the nonprofit sector, a skill she now channels into her speculative fiction, which explores themes of power imbalances and overcoming adversity. Residing in a historic bungalow in Salt Lake City, Michaela enjoys photography, spending time with her family, and advocating for equity in her community.

Elizabeth Suggs

Elizabeth is the co-owner of the indie publisher Collective Tales Publishing, owner of Editing Mee, and author of numerous award-winning stories. Her piece "Into the Dark," featured in the Collective Darkness anthology, was an Amazon Bestseller, and her story "Technicolor Tears" won second place in the Quills Short Story Contest. She is also a book reviewer (EditingMee.com), popular bookstagrammer, and cosplayer (@ElizabethSuggsAuthor). When not writing or reading, she's traveling the world.

Jonathan Reddoch

Jonathan Reddoch is co-owner of Collective Tales Publishing. He is a father, writer, editor, and publisher who creates in genres ranging from sci-fi and fantasy to romance and horror. He has been working on his enormous sci-fi novel for over a decade and hopes to finish it in this lifetime. Find him on Instagram: @jonathanreddochauthor.

Alex Child

Alex Child knows the power of writing but is wise enough to admit he's far from understanding its full potential. Between working half as hard as he should and twice as hard as required at his day job, he continues chasing that indescribable emotional swell that comes from connecting with a literary character. He hopes his story brings you even a portion of that rush.

Joshua G. J. Insole

Three-time Reedsy winner Joshua G. J. Insole is a British writer living in the Austrian Alps. He has published several shortlisted stories, with his debut book released in 2020. Joshua's favored genres are horror and science fiction.

Morgana Price

Morgana Price loves the spooky and the beautiful, often transforming her dark and eerie dreams into stories—much like her contributions to this anthology. As the alter ego of author Alicia Morley Dodson, Morgana draws inspiration from Arthurian legends and the late Vincent Price, whose iconic laugh in Michael Jackson's Thriller still gives her goosebumps (@morganapriceofficial). When she's not writing, she's watching movies, enjoying flora photography, and baking cupcakes.

Robin Knabel

Robin Knabel is a horror author who covers her eyes during scary movies and is the owner/editor of Inky Bones Press. Her short fiction has appeared in various anthologies and magazines, including Exposed Bone Lit Mag, Darkness 101: Lessons Were Learned, The Raven Review, *and* Autumn Noir. *Robin recently published* Dark Decades, *a 6-anthology horror collection, through Inky Bones Press. Her upcoming work will appear in* Darkness 102: Advanced Lessons Were Learned. *Find her at robinknabel.com, where she shares book reviews and photography.*

Edward Suggs

Edward Suggs is an award-winning author. Known for crafting strange and intriguing tales, he aims to inspire readers to look beyond the surface. Outside of writing, Edward expresses his creativity through music, capturing emotions words can't always convey.

Gregory R. Marshall

Gregory R. Marshall writes fiction that confronts injustice, intolerance, and bigotry. He explores the boundaries between fact and fiction, reflecting on how contemporary internet culture and media obscure reality and truth. He is the author of Torn Veil, Fables of Failure, *and the* Rainer series.

Garrett K. Jones

Garrett K. Jones lives in Central California with his family. He holds a BA in Creative Writing from California State University, Monterey Bay, and an MAR in Biblical Studies from Liberty University Theological Seminary. Garrett is currently working on the sixth book in his fantasy series, an undisclosed nonfiction title, and a short story collection. He also hosts the Story Tellers *podcast and co-hosts* War of the Stars (A Star Wars Podcast).

Patrick Moody

Patrick Moody is the author of The Gravedigger's Son *and* Creatures of Clay. *His short fiction has appeared in numerous anthologies, including one set in the H.P. Lovecraft mythos. Several of his stories, such as* A Feast For Saint Hubert *and* The Doctor in the Dungeon, *have been adapted into audio dramas. When not searching for B-horror flicks or participating in historical reenactments, he can be found outside New Haven, Connecticut.*

L. J. Duncan

L. J. Duncan made waves with his controversial Soteria trilogy, which began with End of Pride *in 2020. He continued the dystopian saga with* Dawn of Envy *and* Fall of Wrath. *Based in South Australia with his wife and two daughters, L. J. is an adventurer at heart, believing that a good book offers the same sense of escapism as a wilderness adventure.*

Jennifer Leo

Jennifer Leo's love for storytelling is deeply rooted in her traditional Apache culture. With a long career as a professor of sociology and Native American studies, Jennifer is now exploring sci-fi and fantasy writing from an Indigenous perspective. Her work reflects her passion for both technical writing and creative storytelling.

Jay Seate

Jay Seate's stories span the gamut from horror to humor, with his fiction appearing in Horror Novel Review's Best Short Fiction *and* Chicken Soup for the Soul. *His quirky characters leap off the page, embodying fantasy, suspense, and everything in between.*

Robert Foster

Robert J. Foster is the author of Morgan's Mount *and* Crag Island. *While he writes about dark places, he prefers hiking in green ones. Based in Maine, Robert spent several years teaching English in South Korea, Poland, China, and Taiwan. His next novel is set for release in the winter of 2024.*

Zach Festini

Zach Festini is an independent author from Connecticut. After being introduced to tabletop role-playing games at a young age, his passion for telling good stories flourished into a years-long collection of short fiction. "Blurred" is his first story in print. Always having an affinity toward sci-fi and apocalyptic themes, Zach is working to complete a full-length novel in the coming years. In the meantime, though, you can find him enjoying craft beer, contributing to his Dungeons and Dragons universe, or just out hiking a local trail.

Elizabeth Rayne

Elizabeth Rayne is a creature who writes. Her work has appeared in Ars Technica, Popular Mechanics, SYFY WIRE, *and more. Based just outside New York City with her parrot, Lestat, Elizabeth spends her time drawing, playing piano, or shapeshifting when not writing.*

Elena Boshbozh

Elena Boshbozh is an educator with an MA in English Language and Literature who weaves magical and eerie tales rooted in mythology and folklore. Her writing journey began with The Order of the Horned, *featured in* The Dark Corner Zine. *Elena recently released her debut high fantasy novel* The Sun Under the Earth and The Kingdom Above It *in 2023.*

Stetson Ray

Stetson Ray lives in the hills of East Tennessee and spends most of his time writing. His stories have received multiple awards and prizes, including the Sue Ellen Hudson Award for Excellence in Writing, the James Still Prize for Fiction, and the Jesse Stuart Prize for Young Adult Fiction.Stetson Ray lives in the hills of East Tennessee and spends most of his time writing. His stories have received multiple awards and prizes, including the Sue Ellen Hudson Award for Excellence in Writing, the James Still Prize for Fiction, and the Jesse Stuart Prize for Young Adult Fiction.

WANT MORE?

Check out our current and future anthologies at

www.CTPFiction.com